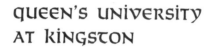

LOCK & KEY

The Secrets of Locking Things Up, In, and Out

LOCK &KEY

Stephen Tchudi

CHARLES SCRIBNER'S SONS · NEW YORK

Maxwell Macmillan Canada · Toronto
Maxwell Macmillan International
New York · Oxford · Singapore · Sydney

Charles Scribner's Sons Books for Young Readers
Macmillan Publishing Company, 866 Third Avenue, New York, NY 10022

Maxwell Macmillan Canada, Inc.
1200 Eglinton Avenue East, Suite 200, Don Mills, Ontario M3C 3N1

Macmillan Publishing Company is part of the
Maxwell Communication Group of Companies.

First edition   10   9   8   7   6   5   4   3   2   1
Printed in the United States of America

Library of Congress Cataloging-in-Publication Data
Tchudi, Stephen, date.
    Lock & key : the secrets of locking things up, in, and out / Stephen Tchudi. —
1st ed.   p.   cm.   Includes bibliographical references and index.
    Summary: Describes the development and uses of different kinds of locks, relates stories about important locks in history, and discusses the meanings that the words "lock" and "key" have taken on in our language.
    ISBN 0-684-19363-9
1. Locks and keys—History—Juvenile literature.
[1. Locks and keys—History.]   I. Title.   II. Title: Lock and key.
TS519.5.T4   1993   683'.3—dc20   92-43252

Acknowledgments

For sharing their considerable knowledge of locks, keys, and security systems, I am grateful to:

Domenic Cicchini, Dom Security Systems, Black & Decker Canada, Brockville, Ontario; Daniel G. Doyle, Computerized Security Systems, Troy, Michigan; Ruth Jacobs and Mike Cunningham, Mosler, Inc., Hamilton, Ohio; Michael Jacobsen, Diebold, Inc., Canton, Ohio; Mark Kelty, Digital Signatures, Inc., Columbia, Maryland; Joseph Kontuly, Telkee, Inc., Glen Riddle, Pennsylvania; Stanley Ross, Abram Friedman Occupational Center, Los Angeles, California; Diana Smoljna, International Security Conference and Exposition, Las Vegas, Nevada; Elaine Snyder and Michelle Kaye, Schlage Lock Company, San Francisco, California; Robert Sterrett, Litton Poly-Scientific, Blacksburg, Virginia; Glen Tarin, The Knox Company, Newport Beach, California; Harriet Thorp, The Kryptonite Corporation, Canton, Massachusetts; William Wilson, Recognition Systems, Inc., San Jose, California; Bob Wright, Master Lock Company, Milwaukee, Wisconsin; Kay V. Youngflesh, National Museum of American History, Smithsonian Institution, Washington, D.C.; The curators of the heavy metal collection, Victoria and Albert Museum, London.

Contents

LOCK &KEY

Foreword

"There's been an accident!" they said,
"Your servant's cut in half; he's dead!"
"Indeed!" said Mr. Jones, "and please
Send me the half that's got my keys."

—Harry Graham (1874–1936)
Ruthless Rhymes for Heartless Homes

At first glance this little poem may seem quite cruel. What kind of person is Mr. Jones that he would care more about his keys than about his servant, who has just been chopped in two in some horrible accident?

Actually Harry Graham's "ruthless rhyme" was written in jest, poking fun at people who only think about their own problems.

But the poem also tells something about locks and keys. Mr. Jones worries about his keys because without them, he's *locked out.* And if you and I lose our keys, we're in trouble. Without the keys to the front door or back door, a locker at school, or a secret diary, our lives become complicated. If he doesn't find the half that has his keys, Mr. Jones may

1

have to become a member of that oldest profession and break into his own home.

Locks and keys of one kind or another are about as ancient as humankind itself. As long as there have been people on earth, there seems to have been a need for locks. Perhaps if human nature were different and people didn't take what doesn't belong to them, we wouldn't need locks and keys. But as things stand, locks and keys have been and are big business. In the United States alone, the security industry sells equipment worth billions of dollars every year just to lock things up, in, or out.

We lock up bicycles, bank vaults, and fence gates; we lock out prowlers and snoopers; we lock in farm animals and criminals. Almost every time we come or go, the first thing we do is open a lock, and the last thing we do is latch it tightly.

As I write I am looking at the key ring I carry around with me. It contains so many keys that it regularly sets off airport security alarms. I have keys to my house—not just one key, but three that fit different doors. Then there are two keys to my car: one that fits the ignition or starter (without that one, I would have to hot-wire my car to get it started), and one that fits the car door and the trunk. My key ring holds a key that locks my bicycle carrier to the top of my car and another key to lock my bike to the carrier. I have a key to my office building, a key that is called a submaster because it will unlock the front door to the building as well as my office, but it won't open every door in the building. And there is a key of mysterious origin, something I clipped on my key ring years ago, a key whose use I've forgotten. I'm afraid to throw it away because it might unlock something important.

If I lost my key ring, I would be temporarily out of work, out of my house, and without my car, so I would have to walk to the locksmith to get control over my own possessions.

Actually, like most people who worry about such things, I carry extra keys, usually in my wallet, so if I happen to lose my car keys or lock my house keys inside, I can regain control of my life.

My wallet also contains some other "unlockers," some modern day "keys." I have a bank card that will unlock the money machine in my neighborhood and let me make withdrawals, provided I have memorized another "key," the personal identification number (or PIN) that tells a computer who I am. I have a telephone credit card that lets me unlock the long-distance phone system. And I have a YMCA identification card with a striped bar code that will open an electronically locked door to the locker room when I run it through a scanning device.

Now that I've finished this guided tour of my pockets, you might look at the keys you carry around. Or if you don't carry keys, at least explore the place where you are reading—home, classroom, library, bus—looking for locks. You may be surprised to realize that you pass by hundreds, possibly thousands, of locks every day.

Locks and keys come in a marvelous array of sizes, shapes, mechanical workings, and prices. You can buy tiny padlocks for a quarter from a gum ball machine, locks so weak you can possibly pick them with a paper clip. At the larger end of the scale is a record-holding padlock called Ivan the Terrible, a twenty-pounder that the *Guinness Book of World Records* says is the world's largest. Throughout history locksmiths have created amazing and intricate locks and keys: keys that work like screws, locks with locked keyholes requiring a second key, strongboxes with as many as twenty locks, push-button locks with no keys, keys that are as big as your arm (see Figures 1 and 2), keys so small you can wear them on a charm bracelet.

As Louis Zara has written in his book *Locks and Keys:*

> Together or separately [locks and keys] are part of man's cultural heritage and deserve as much attention as the wheel, the clock, the steam engine, the camera, the internal combustion motor, or any other invention.

Locks and keys are part of our culture, locked in to our myths, legends, and superstitions. For example in England it was believed that a sick person could not die as long as you left the doors of the house locked to prevent the escape of the soul. However death, as William Shakespeare wrote, is the "sure Physician" with the "key to unbar these doors."

On a more positive note Russians believed that a key held in your hand would stop bleeding from a wound, and the Scottish people would place a key behind the neck to stop a nosebleed. Germans have worn keys as charms to ward off "the evil eye." In China people have been given keys at birth, and they wear these throughout life as a way of locking themselves into happy circumstances.

In religions all over the world gods and goddesses are said to hold the keys to human happiness. Jesus told his followers, "I will give you the keys to the kingdom of heaven." St. Peter is said to hold the keys to the heavenly gates, and whether or not you get into heaven is determined by whether or not Peter opens the gate for you. In ancient Babylonia

FIGURE 1. A four-hundred-year-old lock from a cathedral in Austria. *Schlage Lock Company*

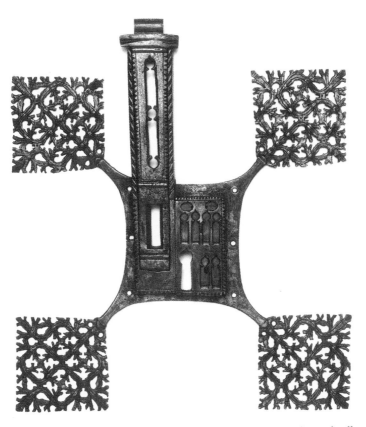

FIGURE 2. An Italian lock from the fifteenth century. *Victoria and Albert Museum, London*

Marduk was a powerful god who controlled the lesser gods and imprisoned the evil ones; he also held the keys to the kingdom of heaven. In Mesopotamia, Ishtar was the queen of the universe; she held no fewer than seven keys to unlock the gates of the underworld. In Greek mythology the goddess Athena carried the keys to the city of Athens, while Hecate's key ring included the keys to the universe. Also in Greek mythology Hades held the keys to the underworld, where evil souls were sent for punishment. In Roman mythology the god Janus was in charge of comings and goings, and he is shown in paintings with two faces: one each for departings and arrivals, for locking and unlocking.

In this book I'll look at the secrets and fascination of locks and keys, from wooden latches to modern electronic fasteners. I'll show you how locks and keys work as miniature machines, and I will examine odd and curious keys and locks developed for unusual purposes. We'll see how the words *lock* and *key* have become an important part of our language, and we'll read stories about some of history's great locks, locksmiths, and lockpicks.

In his book *Liberal Education* Thomas Huxley wrote that a person who can read has "the keys to the great wisdom box." You, the reader, have the reading key that will unlock this book. Turn the pages. Unlock the secrets of *Lock & Key*.

1

Unlocking the History of Locks

Nobody knows who invented the first lock, when it happened, or where it occurred. Many historians suppose that locksmithing began in the days of the cave dwellers. We can imagine that the first lockmaker was a person who returned from foraging or hunting to find that his cave had been raided, perhaps by animals, possibly by people. To protect his property, he got the idea of placing a stone, the biggest one he could move, over the mouth of the cave, thus hiding the cave entrance and blocking—or locking—it against unwanted entry. He may have discovered that this "lock" worked well with animals, which couldn't figure out the "key" to getting into the cave.

However, other cave dwellers quickly learned to "pick" this "lock." All they had to do was roll or drag the rock away. Two people working together could easily move a rock placed by a single person, even a strong one. So, our cave dweller might use an even bigger rock, asking his friends or family to help place it. Aside from the fact that this huge stone would make for an incredibly awkward front door, the caveman's enemies could still use even more of *their* allies to remove it.

Historians suppose that our cave dweller next tried the trick of wedging a smaller stone beneath the large one, just as an object wedged under an automobile tire prevents a car from rolling downhill. This arrangement made it difficult to roll the larger rock. Once again, however, the raiders might be able to figure out this trick, or key, and simply move the smaller, wedged-in stone. A battle of wits between the locksmiths and the lock-picks had begun, a battle that continues to this day.

Our cave dweller-lockmaker might have tried other strategies. Instead of rolling ever-more-weighty rocks that tested his strength, he might have created a barrier with tree limbs or trunks, locking this simple gate with a rudimentary latch or a network of sticks. Or he might have invented a trap, rigging a large rock or a tree limb to fall on an intruder, crushing him. Sooner or later, however, the other cave people would learn these secrets. They might make a "key" out of a long pole and use it to set off the trap from a safe distance.

The wars between lockmakers and lockpicks thus continued.

Historians imagine too that, during prehistory, people might have locked themselves *in* for protection against animals or human enemies, using systems of vines or homemade ropes to fasten the doors of huts or caves. It is likely too that as humans learned to raise animals for food, they figured out ways to lock their animals inside fences, perhaps using locks of rope or latches made from wood.

Locking Up the Treasures

When we arrive at the time of written history, we learn of other interesting ways of locking things up, in, and out. In ancient India the emperor of Annam is reported to have made a system of "living locks." He placed his valuable gold and jewels on small islands in a moat. Then he released crocodiles in the water. And he didn't feed the crocs all that often. So his "locks" were always on the prowl for a good meal. The thief who wanted to get at the emperor's treasure would have to brave the man-eating crocodiles to get at the goods. One can imagine that this croc-lock was quite effective. Of course there was the problem of how the emperor himself could get at his own possessions. The story goes that he would drug the crocs so servants could safely retrieve the gold and jewels. Of course it would be possible for a thief to use the same strategy, ''picking'' the lock by drugging the crocodiles.

We read too of Egyptian rulers who locked their treasures in deep vaults, heavily guarded. In fact, there were even places that served as safe-deposit vaults. The ruler would deposit his treasure, in boxes sealed with wax, behind great doors that were protected round-the-clock by teams of guards. When the noble came back, he would carefully inspect the seals to see that they were not broken, thus assuring him that nobody had touched the treasure.

Heavy rocks . . . tree limbs . . . ropes . . . crocodiles . . . wax seals. These may not seem much like the locks and keys we have today, but in them you can see the beginnings of our modern-day security systems.

A lock, after all, is simply a barrier or closure, a way of sealing up an entryway, of keeping what you want in, *in,* what you want out, *out.* A key is a device for opening the gates or door. The person who creates a lock holds the secret or the key, and anyone who wants to penetrate the lock has to figure out the secret or obtain the key. Strictly speaking, hiding your money in a mattress or in a cookie jar or behind the encyclopedia is a way of locking it up from burglars, though not a very safe one. A stick or doorstop that you wedge under a door to keep out your parents or younger brothers and sisters is also a lock, though, again, not a reliable or unpickable one.

In his book *All About Locks and Locksmithing* Max Alth has remarked that ''locks are puzzles, little machines, footnotes to history. . . .'' A key is ''something that gives an explanation or provides a solution.'' Even in the early lock systems we see human ingenuity at work, both in creating lock puzzles and in figuring out answers that unlock.

The Wooden Pin Lock

Max Alth also writes that ''the locksmithing profession is now in its fifth millennium,'' that is, it is five thousand years old. The earliest known

locks and keys that resemble modern-day locks can be traced back to
Egypt and Persia; they were made as early as 3000 B.C.

In 1842 Paul Emile Botta, a French archaeologist, was digging in the
remains of the palace of Emperor Sargon II in Khorsabad, Persia. The
palace, which Sargon occupied from about 722 to 705 B.C., covered about
twenty-five acres of ground. Botta estimated that as many as eighty thousand people must have lived within its walls. Professor Botta also discovered the remains of a huge wooden gate. Looking at the mechanism
of the bolt—the bar that keeps a gate closed—he could figure out that
it had been opened by a key.

A very large wooden key, it turns out—it was the size of a modern-
day baseball bat. The person with the key would slide it into an arm-
sized hole in the gate, and if pegs sticking up on the key matched holes
and pegs in the hole, the door would open. In fact the key itself would
serve as a giant handle to move the bolt.

Other researchers have found drawings of similar keys at the Egyptian
temple at Karnak, thus confirming Professor Botta's ideas. In fact a few
wooden keys made from teak—a hard wood that does not decay easily—
have been found in the tombs of Egyptian kings at Luxor. Some of the
keys had elegant ivory handles decorated with gold and silver, and it is
supposed that the Egyptian kings would have their keys entombed with
them when they died.

It's interesting to see how these locks and keys worked, for it turns
out they are surprisingly similar to many modern systems. Craftspeople
at the Smithsonian Institution in Washington, D.C., have created a model
of these early locks. Figure 3 shows the model disassembled. The key is
shaped something like a toothbrush, with pegs where the bristles would
be. The pegs on the key match sliding pegs that rest in holes inside the
lock. (These sliders are shown hanging down at the left of the photograph.) When the sliders are in the down position, they slip into holes
and prevent the bolt or latch of the door from moving.

Figure 4 shows the lock assembled. The key slides into an opening,
where its pegs line up with the down-sliding pegs. The key then lifts the
slider pegs, and the key itself serves as a handle to move the bolt. To

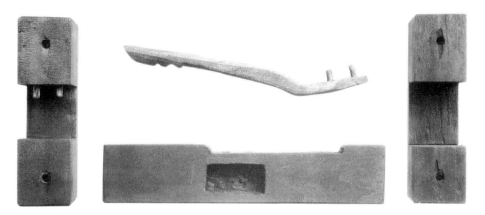

FIGURE 3. The parts of an Egyptian pin lock. *Smithsonian Institution*

FIGURE 4. Egyptian pin lock assembled. *Smithsonian Institution*

create a more complicated lock, a person could have more sliding and lifting pegs, make them of differing lengths, and arrange them in designs or patterns. That way each lock and key would be unique—one key would fit only one lock.

Of course this lock would not be too difficult to pick. You could slide your fingers or a long stick into the slot to fiddle with the sliders and thus release the bolt. A lock made of wood could also be damaged or destroyed by fire or with a hammer or ax. Still, these locks were a big improvement over rocks and vines. The Bible mentions locks for the

FIGURE 5. A wooden pin lock from the Dutch East Indies. *Schlage Lock Company*

house of King David and states that the builders "set up the doors thereof, and the locks thereof, and the bars thereof." It's a pretty good bet that the locks were wooden pin locks.

Despite their weaknesses, wooden pin locks are easy and inexpensive to make, and they have continued to be used in many countries up to modern times. Wooden pin locks have been found in almost every part of the world—in Morocco in Africa, in the Faroe Islands north of Scotland, in England, France, Japan, and Norway. Figure 5 shows a modern wooden pin lock from the Dutch East Indies. The handle of the key is carved in the shape of a rooster's head, for the rooster is sometimes called "the security officer of the barnyard," crowing to raise a fuss whenever anything unusual happens.

The Greek and Roman Locks

The Tigris and Euphrates rivers of the Middle East are sometimes called "the cradle of civilization," because much of our culture in the Western world grew from that area. Many of our ideas about religion started there, as did our alphabet and the roots of language. The palace of Sargon, where Professor Botta discovered the evidence of wooden locks, was also on the banks of the Tigris River.

As was true of religion and culture and language, ideas about locks and keys reached our part of the world by passing through Greece and then Rome.

We know that about 1000 B.C. Greek locksmiths were in business, figuring out new ways to bar the doors. They were experimenting with a much more durable substance than wood: metal. A famous story by the Greek poet Homer tells of the journeys and battles of Odysseus. One verse in the poem describes a key used by Penelope, the wife of Odysseus, to open the treasure room:

> Penelope took a crooked key in her firm hand, a goodly key of bronze, having an ivory handle. She loosed the strap, thrust in the key, and with careful aim shot back the door bolt.

We know from materials found in ruins that the key Penelope used was probably shaped like a sickle, a curved letter C, perhaps twelve inches or longer. (See Figure 6.) Such keys were so awkward that servants carried them around to save their masters sweat and strain.

In an advancement over the wooden pin lock, the Greeks developed the idea of a keyhole, so the sickle-shaped key could be inserted in the hole from outside and thrust into the innards of the door where it would hook and open the bolt. Because of the curve of the key, one couldn't use just any stick to trigger the mechanism. Once the latch had been "tickled" by this key, the bolt could be moved.

Actually, these Greek locks were pretty unsophisticated compared to the simplest door lock in modern times. To pick a Greek lock, one simply needed a bent rod roughly like the sickle-shaped key, perhaps with a little hook on the end to lift the latch. Therefore the nobility, like Penelope, also had guards on hand to watch over the treasure, not trusting their fortunes completely to the locks.

The Romans are credited with an important advancement in making locks more secure: the ward. You may have heard the expression, to "ward off" evil spirits. The word simply means "to guard" or "to protect." The ward on a Roman lock was meant to defend against something more earthly than spirits; it was designed to fend off a human lockpick. The Romans warded their locks in two ways. First, they created keyholes in odd or unusual shapes: Xs, stars, other patterns. Unless your key was shaped in the pattern, you couldn't get your key into the keyhole and you were warded off. Second, inside the lock, the Roman lockmaker would put strips of metal to block any key not cut to the right shape. Thus even if one could get the wrong key in the lock, the lock mechanism itself wouldn't open.

Unfortunately, most of the Roman locks were made of iron, and they have rusted away over the centuries. What we know about Roman locks must be based on looking at bronze keys, which were a little more rust resistant. Archaeologists have found Roman keys shaped like small

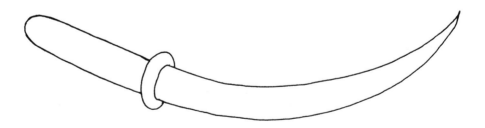

FIGURE 6. A Greek "sickle-shaped" key, probably about a foot long.

rakes or pitchforks, fishhooks, even four-pronged boat anchors. (See Figure 7.)

Many of the keys came with holes in the handles, and it is supposed that the Romans wore keys as rings on their fingers or tied the keys around their necks with string. (Roman togas, those sheetlike garments, had no pockets to carry keys.)

Because the Romans were travelers (they conquered what was then most of the known world—from Egypt to Greece to France to England), they had a need for locks that could be carried around, not just sunk into doors. The Romans made important contributions to locksmithery by developing portable locks, the forerunners of today's padlocks.

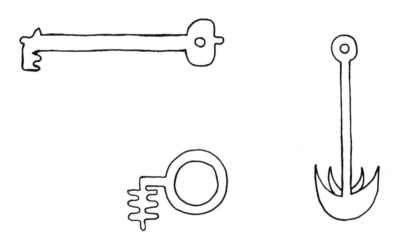

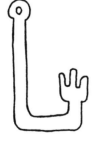

FIGURE 7. Roman keys, sketched from the collections at the Victoria and Albert Museum, London, and the Schlage Museum, San Francisco. The tip, or bit, of the key fits around wards inside the lock. Holes in the handle, or bow, are for carrying the key with string or on one's finger.

Nevertheless, despite the advancements, the Roman locks were easily picked. A slim piece of metal or wire could bypass the warded keyhole and the internal wards and flip open the lock.

Locksmithing in the Middle Ages

From Rome locksmithing spread into Europe, then to England. For well over a thousand years, there were no major changes in how locks worked. The locksmith of the Middle Ages was actually a blacksmith too. He would heat iron red-hot, then pound it into shape with a hammer. At first blacksmith locks were not very sophisticated. However, as time passed and traditions of 'smithing were passed along, locksmiths became very clever about ways to trick, confuse, or slow down lockpicks. A famous collector of locks, Vincent Eras, wrote that the aim was

> to provide the keys with the most complicated bits and, at the same time, to incorporate in to the lock mechanisms all sorts of obstructions fitting in and around the keyhole.

In other words the keys became more and more complicated to fit more and more complex locks. On the outside, keyholes were cut to special shapes to keep out all but the right key. On the inside more and more bands of metal required a more intricate key shape. Figure 8 shows a lock that was made in France in the fifteenth century. The bit (the part of the key that goes into the lock) has a number of cuts to fit around complicated metal bands inside the lock.

You can see too that locks and keys were becoming very elaborate. Locksmiths were beginning to see their craft as an art. They learned new ways of shaping metal, using tools such as fine saws, files, and chisels, not just the blacksmith's heavy, crude hammer. They learned to work with thinner pieces of metal, and they created combination metals, called alloys, that could be kneaded and bent in new ways. The new techniques let them construct the innards and outards of locks with much more complexity. Interestingly, at this time many blacksmiths-locksmiths also were making armor for knights, and some of the fancier metal

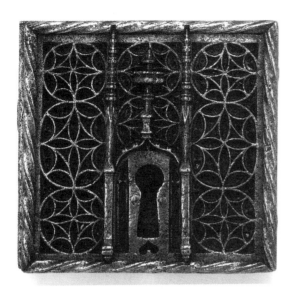

FIGURE 8. Fifteenth-century French lock. *Victoria and Albert Museum, London*

suits—the costume for a knight in shining armor—were created at the same time as the elaborate locks and keys you see in this book.

Of course doing such elaborate metal work was very time-consuming. Locks and keys could not be mass-produced, stamped out by a machine. Each lock was one-of-a-kind and so was each key. The apprenticeship system helped to make this high art of the lock possible. The master lockmaker would have a number of boys apprenticed to him. Their purpose was to learn the craft, but in fact they would do much of the simple work (and the dirty, boring work) of lockmaking. Once a lad became sufficiently skilled, he could join the lockmaker's guild, or union, and go into business for himself.

As a final examination for his apprenticeship, the boy would often be asked to create what was called a masterpiece lock, an incredibly complicated and detailed lock and key. One masterpiece lock that survived to our time has been stripped down to its basic parts. Historians estimate that using the fairly simple tools of the Middle Ages, an apprentice might have spent three thousand hours making a single lock. If you worked forty hours per week, that would be eighteen months out of your life. Of course a person who had no patience or was clumsy or sloppy could never last out an apprenticeship and would move on to another craft or trade.

The locks not only became fancier as works of art, but trickier in methods of operating. Although the mechanism of a warded lock could be picked by a person of some skill, locksmiths developed ways of making it more and more difficult to get lockpicking tools into the lock. Keyholes were covered with flaps, or gateways, and the entryway could be hidden in the curlicues of the artwork, making it as difficult to find the keyhole as to pick the lock.

Figure 9 shows a characteristic lock from the time, one found at a

FIGURE 9. German castle lock. *Schlage Lock Company*

German castle. It had five spring latches and a complex system of wards to prevent entry by unauthorized keys. The keyhole itself was hidden in the dome of the lock, which was elaborately decorated with dragonlike animals and a minstrel playing a stringed instrument.

Still another technique to make lock systems more secure was simply to use more locks. If it required, say, twenty minutes for a person to pick a lock, putting two locks on a door or cabinet would require forty minutes, increasing the probability that the thief would be caught in the act. Princess Isabelle of Bavaria created a system of five locks to protect her ladies-in-waiting. King Henry II of France ordered a set of three locks for the chamber of his mistress. Each of Henry's locks used a different set of wards and keys, but the king himself had a master key that would work in all three locks.

Locks on treasure chests became enormously complicated, sometimes with as many as twelve different locks. Lifting the lid, you would find the whole inside filled with a network of levers and gears for this locking system, whose keyholes were all hidden in the decorations on the outside of the chest. (See Figure 10.) A Frenchman, Monsieur de Réaumer, studied one of these chests and observed that

> . . . nothing is wanting in these chests in the score of solidarity. They are made entirely of iron, or if of wood, they are banded both within and without with iron, and can be broken open only with great violence. Their locks are almost as large as the top of the coffer and close with a great number of bolts.

False keyholes were placed on the lids of some of these chests, causing a lockpick to waste time fiddling with a keyhole to nowhere. Spring-loaded keyhole covers would open only if you knew special places to push.

In fact some of these cases were even rigged as *traps* for the unwary. Holes in the cover of a case were conveniently designed to look like finger grips for use in raising the lid. However, spring-loaded metal jaws lurked inside the holes, ready to mangle the fingers of a thief who didn't know the secret. One lock of the period was even designed with a spring-loaded

FIGURE 10. Lock mechanism in the lid of a German "treasure" chest.

dart, so if you failed to work the lock in exactly the right way, you were likely to be zinged by the dart. The Marquis of Wooster described a design that

> seteth an alarum a-going, which the stranger cannot stop . . . ; and besides, though none shall be within hearing, yet it catcheth his hand as a trap doth a fox; and though far from maiming him, yet it leaveth such a mark behind it as will discover him if suspected.

When locks were so complicated and even dangerous, there were a couple of other ways to steal treasures. One was simply to seize the whole chest, haul it away, and work on it with a large hammer called a maul. Another strategy was simply to bypass the lock system and attack the chest at a weaker spot. One writer in the 1500s saw someone who "pull[ed] out the nayles of the hindges and opened hit [a chest] on the other side, contrary to the locke."

As we will see in coming chapters, burglars will often bypass rather than try to open a really good lock. It's easier to break down a door or

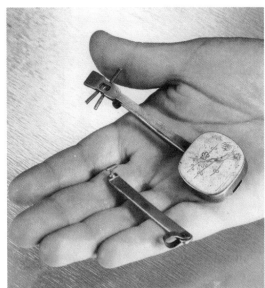

FIGURE 11. An eighteenth-century Indian temple padlock. *Schlage Lock Company*

FIGURE 12. A Japanese slide-key padlock. *Schlage Lock Company*

blow the door off a safe than to pick the lock. Of course lockmakers take a certain kind of pride when this happens: It's not the lock that failed, but some other weaker structure like the door or the "hindges."

Locks in Other Lands

Because so much of our Western history comes to us from Rome, it is easy for us to forget that technology developed in different parts of the world. There are many ways in which one can build a lock to open or close whenever you want. Samples of locks found in Middle Eastern and Eastern countries, from Persia to China, show other kinds of machinery. Some locks have a screw-type key: Only a key with the right pattern of threads will pop loose the hasp or open the bolt.

Many countries regarded locks and keys as works of art. For example,

FIGURE 13. A Russian pad-
lock. *Smithsonian Institution*

a pair of bronze padlocks made for the Chinese emperor K'ang-hsi are
carved with beautiful dragons, symbolizing the emperor's power, and
engraved with important dates in Chinese history. Locks and keys from
India are made in the shape of Hindu gods, scorpions, horses, and dogs.
There are locks that look like fish, hearts, dragons, and almost any animal
of interest to people. Locks have been built as puzzles or games, and
locks with dials—the forerunners of combination locks—are actually
well over a thousand years old.

Figure 11 shows a lovely lock from India that is opened with a cone-
shaped key. The lock is created in the shape of a woman carrying a *matka,*
or water vessel, on her head. But the art also hides the trickery of the
lock, for you have to unscrew the *matka* to discover the keyway or
keyhole. Then the key tool is inserted to spring open four clasps or latches.

Figure 12 shows yet another kind of locking mechanism as well as
high artistry and craftsmanship. This Japanese lock is made to look like

a musical instrument called a *samisen*. It uses a slide key, which is inserted into the lock and compresses some springs that, in turn, let the bolt pop open.

In Russia the empress Catherine the Great, who ruled from 1762 to 1796, was deeply interested in locks and developed an extensive collection. Figure 13 shows a lock believed to be from Catherine's collection. It is a large padlock with a very complex system of wards. Notice that the tip, or bit, of the key has several cross-shaped cuts to get around the barriers inside the lock. But if you look at the keyhole, you see that the key itself had to be shaped like a cross just to get into the keyhole. It's a wonderful piece of evidence that locksmithing is an art known all around the world.

2 The War Between Locksmiths and Lockpicks

For the first four thousand years of locksmithing, locks were simply not very secure. With a warded lock—the kind made by the Romans and the craftsmen of the Middle Ages—any person who knew how locks worked could, with time, pick a lock. A thin piece of metal could penetrate almost any oddly shaped keyhole. A skeleton key, with a simple bit, could bypass many complicated ward systems. (See Figure 14.) It seemed that no matter how clever the lockmaker was in disguising or tricking up the lock, a lockpick would be able to conquer the system.

In the middle of the 1700s, however, things began to change. In England the population was growing rapidly, especially in the cities. Crime was on the increase. Burglaries were common, and people wanted better ways of protecting their goods.

At about the same time, the world was beginning to enter what we now call the machine age. Steam engines were developed, and craftsmen were able to apply these engines to many jobs, cutting down on hand labor. For the locksmith the machine age brought not only changes, but new possibilities for security. Now, instead of making every single lock

"GUESS WHAT, MR. WILSON! MY JUNIOR DETECTIVE SKELETON KEY OPENS YOUR BACK DOOR!"

FIGURE 14. Dennis the Menace®, used by permission of Hank Ketcham and © by North America Syndicate.

by hand, and each lock different, or one-of-a-kind, a lockmaker could use machines to stamp out or press a number of identical parts in a short period of time.

During a one-hundred-year period, English lockmakers invented numerous new locking systems, each time seeking a patent that would prevent others from using or stealing the idea. These new patent locks proved to be much stronger and much more secure than those of the Middle Ages. Now, instead of simply trying to foil a lockpick with secret keyholes or darts, the lockmakers set out to create an unpickable lock.

The New "Tumbler" Locks: Barron and Bramah

One breakthrough came in the work of Robert Barron, who, in 1778, took out a patent for what he called a "lever-tumbler" lock. Instead of simply putting in wards, or barriers, Barron used a series of moving levers, or tumblers, in his lock. Inside the lock case were a series of bars or levers lined up side by side. When the levers were in line with one another, the bolt of a door would be blocked from moving—locked, in other words. When the proper key was inserted in the lock, each lever would be raised a certain amount, lining up small notches in the levers. That, in turn, created a "gate" in all the levers so that the bolt could move—the door was unlocked.

With power machine tools, the manufacturer could stamp out levers that were identical, *except* for the placement of the gate, or slot. The lockmaker could thus make many different locks, all looking the same but each one opening with a different key. Also, the more levers you stacked within the lock, the more complicated the key, and the more difficult it would be to pick the lock. In theory, you could make a lock with dozens of levers. Such a lock would have a long, narrow key. It would be complex and expensive to make, but it would be virtually unpickable.

Most of the early Barron locks contained four or five levers, creating a lock that was difficult to pick and not too expensive.

Still, a Barron lock *could* be picked by a process known as "tickling." The lockpicker would insert a thin piece of metal in the lock and wiggle or fiddle each lever in turn until all the levers were lined up and the lock would open. Right away, lockmakers began working on ways of making tickling more difficult. One version of a Barron lever-tumbler lock was spring-loaded; if a lever was raised too high, the lever would snap down and prevent further tampering. Only the proper key would raise the levers to the right height and thus avoid triggering the spring. Another lock was designed to seize and hold a key that wasn't just right. However, these improvements simply meant that a lockpick would need to be more gentle in tickling. The locks could still be picked.

In 1784 Joseph Bramah developed the next improvement in locks. He worked out a complicated system of sliders inside his locks. Only when a person used the right key would notches in the sliders line up in such a way as to let the locking mechanism turn.

But his first locks weren't foolproof either, and Joseph Bramah was discouraged to read ads in London newspapers in which locksmiths would offer to pick a Bramah lock if an owner had lost a key. The 'smiths were using thin forceps, or tweezers, to penetrate the lock and raise the levers.

For many years Joseph Bramah worked to improve this lock. He eventually designed one he felt confident in advertising as "Impregnable as the Rock of Gibraltar." In 1811 he offered a reward of two hundred guineas (considerably more than two hundred dollars, an extraordinary sum in those days) to anybody who could pick the lock. A British writer explained:

> The principle of the Bramah lock appeared so perfect and unassailable, that for 50 years a padlock . . . hung in a shop window in Piccadilly with a board attached, on which was inscribed, "The artist who can make an instrument to pick this lock shall receive 200 guineas the moment it is produced."

Piccadilly is a busy square in London, with thousands of people passing by every day; yet for years no one accepted the challenge. (Later in this chapter you will learn how the lock came to be removed from the shop window and the two hundred guineas paid.) It is said the improved Bramah lock was so secure that if owners now lost a key, they simply removed the whole lock from their door and bought a new one, for no locksmith in the city could fashion a new key or pick the lock.

The Chubb Locks

The next development in locks came about through the creativity of the three Chubb brothers, whose name is still carried by one of England's most famous lock companies. In 1818 Charles, Jeremiah, and John Chubb took out a patent for a new lever-style lock with several antipick devices. (See Figure 15.)

Joseph Bramah criticized the Chubb lock, claiming it was weakly constructed and would wear out rapidly. The Chubbs responded to this challenge by connecting the lock to a small engine that opened it 460,000 times. When the lock was taken apart, it showed no signs of wear.

Some lockpicks had early success in picking a Chubb lock through a process called "smoking." A flame inserted into the keyhole smoked the bottoms of the levers, thus allowing the picker to obtain a pattern to make a false key or picking tool. But the Chubbs added a revolving metal curtain, or screen, that warded off false keys and lockpicking tools and protected the bottoms of the levers against smoking. Some Chubb locks also contained a detector mechanism that showed an owner when the lock levers had been raised above key height, indicating that the lock had been tampered with.

At about this time the English government was so concerned about the increasing numbers of burglaries that it offered a prize of one hundred pounds (another hefty sum) to anyone who could create an unpickable lock. A Chubb lock was entered in the competition. A lockpick who had been idling away his days in a British prison boasted that he could pick any lock. He was offered the one hundred pounds plus his freedom if he

FIGURE 15. A Chubb lock. The cover has been removed to show the internal parts. *Smithsonian Institution*

could open the Chubb. He toiled away at the task for over three months but failed, leaving the Chubb lock as the champion of the industry and the convict behind bars. History does not record the brand of the lock on his cell.

Picking the Unpickable

There is a saying in the lock business: "The locksmiths are only a half step ahead of the lockpicks." As soon as lockmakers create a new design, lockpicks set to work figuring out how to get in, through, or past the new lock.

So it was with the Chubb lock, although a third of a century passed before the unpickable was plucked.

In 1851 England hosted an International Industrial Exhibition at London's Crystal Palace hall. New machinery and equipment from all over the world was on display, including locks. At the exposition an American, Charles Hobbs, challenged the Chubb Company. In front of witnesses, and using some simple tools he had constructed himself, Hobbs picked a Chubb lock within twenty-five minutes.

The lock world was even more amazed when Hobbs then set about to pick the Bramah lock that had hung for years in the Piccadilly shop window. He worked for four hours per day using another of his home-made tools, a thin balance rod with a small weight on the end. By inserting the rod in the lock, he was able to tickle the levers, also using the weight as a sort of "third hand" to keep pressure on the levers. On the tenth day, again in front of witnesses, he showed that he had opened the Bramah lock. There were no scratches or dents on the lock case, proof that he had picked the lock, not opened the casing. Hobbs also showed that the lock mechanism was still in fine operating condition, which indicated that he had picked it cleanly, not simply broken or bent the levers. The Bramah lock company paid the two hundred guineas. They also went back to the drawing board and made improvements in the lock to make it less pickable. Of course you could still say that if it took a man of Hobbs's skill ten days to open the lock, it was quite secure for ordinary purposes.

Later the Chubb Company hired Hobbs to work for them, figuring, correctly, that since he was such a great lockpick, he could also help them figure out new and more secure designs for their locks.

The Chubb Company became the number one lockmaker in England. A poem on a Chubb Company calendar boasted of how a Chubb lock could make Britons feel secure during the darkening month of November:

> Once more the year revolves to long dark nights
> The burglar's pick the lonely house invites;
> But you may soundly sleep, sure as a rock
> Impregnable, through Chubb's detector lock.

In 1859, just a few years after Charles Hobbs had humbled the company by picking its lock, Chubb received the following, rather satisfying letter from, of all people, a burglar:

> Sir:
>
> I am 55 years of age and spent 35 years of my life as a burglar. I have opened many kinds of locks in my career as a criminal, yet I have never known any burglar who has successfully opened a Chubb mortice deadlock, myself included.
>
> You can take it from me that your lock is definitely invulnerable to light fingered gentlemen of my profession.

Forty years later, Chubb was still making secure locks, and the company even claimed a role in the emancipation of women. The modern woman of 1898 didn't want to stay home cooking, sewing, and cleaning. A Chubb lock supposedly gave her the peace of mind to go out, riding another new device that was giving freedom to daring women: the bicycle.

THE NEW WOMAN 1898

> A modern spinster I
> With latch key for my Chubb;
> I roll my cigarette,
> And cycle to my club.

(Notice, too, the mention of a cigarette in this poem. Smoking was also seen as a symbol of the modern woman.)

The English lockmakers—Barron, Bramah, Chubb, and others—brought a new level of security to England. They also created a flourishing lock industry. Although much of the work was now done by machines, a great deal of lockmaking was still done by hand, and it was hard, even painful work.

The town of Willenhall was known as the center of the lock industry. In 1841 it reported having 268 locksmiths, 76 key makers, and 27 people making door bolts or latches. Over one thousand boys were serving as apprentice locksmiths in this city, some of them as young as seven years of age. Boys were brought to the shops as soon as they were tall enough to reach the workbenches, and sometimes even earlier, when they would be given boxes to stand on to raise them to the benches. These boys and men worked long hours, sometimes sixteen hours a day. A writer visiting Willenhall observed that the workers would barely stop to eat lunch:

> You see the locksmith and his two apprentices, with a plate before each of them heaped up . . . with potatoes and lumps of something or other, but seldom meat, and a large slice of bread in one hand; your attention is called off for a few minutes and on turning round again, you see the men and boys filing at the vice.

The men and boys of Willenhall worked so long and hard that over time, many of them developed twisted, crippled bodies from leaning over the vise, hunched up, making locks and keys. Because of their humped backs, the whole district eventually became known as Humpshire.

Made in the U.S.A.

Not all the developments in locksmithing were taking place in England. From the founding of the United States of America until 1920, approximately three thousand patents for locking devices, gizmos, and gadgets

were filed with the government. Among these were patents for yet another new lock, the pin tumbler lock that became the standard for locks
and is still the most commonly used lock today.

Many American craftsmen turned their hand to lockmaking in the
early days of the new nation. As it had been in the Middle Ages, many
locksmiths were also blacksmiths, pounding out locks that may not have
been sophisticated, but were good enough to keep the cows at home and
the burglars out.

Many inventors were at work in America as well, fiddling and fussing
to make better locks. In 1836 Solomon Andrews, an inventor-lockmaker
from Perth Amboy, New Jersey, developed a lock whose internal levers
could be changed or rearranged. With this lock the owner could actually
change the lock pattern if he or she lost the key or thought someone had
taken an impression.

A locksmith named Perkins of Newbury, Massachusetts, developed a
bank lock that used round disks, or washers, for its tumblers. By changing
the stack of washers, one could also change the keys required to enter.
And the Herring Company created a handy little lock called The Grass-
hopper: When the lock handle was turned, the key hopped out of the
lock and into the user's hand.

The Newell and Day Company of New York created especially interesting locks, perhaps because one of their employees was Charles Hobbs,
the man who, in 1851, went to England and picked the Bramah and
Chubb locks. In 1836 Newell and Day created a changeable lock with
three different sets of inner mechanisms. (See Figure 16.) As a precaution
the levers were set away from the keyhole, making it difficult for a
lockpick to get tools into the guts of the lock. The company called this
elaborate lock the Parautoptic, from the Greek, meaning "hidden from
sight." In the spirit of the age the company put up a cash prize for anybody
who could pick the lock. In 1851 a man named Garbutt made an effort
and worked at the task for thirty days. He had to give up. His failure was
due to the complexity of the key, which had ten different indentations,
or cuts. Some people estimated that to pick a lock with that many levers
would require years of work. To complicate matters even more, the New-

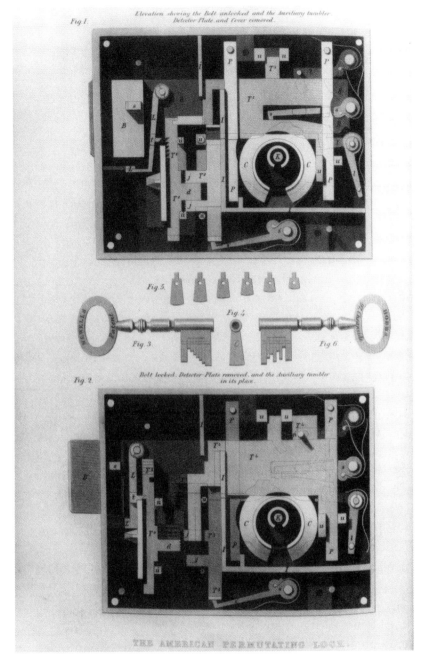

FIGURE 16. A Newell and Day lock. The drawings of the keys show how the bits could be rearranged to allow the lock to be changed. *Smithsonian Institution*

ell and Day Company also made a Permutating lock that featured changeable keys.

The Yale Locks

Enter Linus Yale, Sr., followed by Linus Yale, Jr.

In 1853 Linus Yale the elder patented a new kind of lock that used
pins rather than levers to block the movement of the bolt. Interestingly
enough, the design was similar in principle to the wooden pin locks
described in chapter 1. A pin lock contains an inner metal cylinder, or
plug, which turns inside a larger cylinder by means of a key. Small pins
are pushed down by springs from the outer cylinder into the plug. When
the pins are down, the plug cannot turn. When the proper key is inserted
in the lock, the pins are raised to just the right height, allowing the lock
to turn.

Actually, it's a bit more complicated than that. As Figure 17 shows,
each pin is actually two pins (or one pin cut in two unequal lengths).
When the key is inserted in the lock, the pins are raised so that the break
or cut between pins lines up exactly with the junction of the plug
and the outer cylinder, creating what's called a "shear line." At that
moment the plug can turn in the cylinder, allowing the lock to open.

The first Yale locks used a flat key, which, in turn, made it possible for
a lockpick to use a simple flat piece of metal to get at the lock. Enter
Linus Yale the younger, who introduced several new ideas, including
zigzag keyways. (Pin tumbler locks don't have key*holes;* the thin slit in
a lock is now called a key*way.*) These keyways worked even better than
the old warded keyholes, because now a blank key with a special shape
was needed just to get into the lock. (If you look at just about any lock
today you will see that the zigzag keyway is still in use. Each modern-
day lock company has a particular pattern of zigs and zags for its locks
and key blanks.) (See Figure 18.)

The Yale company also knew that thieves who couldn't pick a lock
would sometimes drill out the plug. To thwart this technique, they placed
drillproof hardened steel bearings, tiny balls, in the lock at the point of

entry. (Drilling out a lock is a technique that is still used today, by the way. If you lose the key to a safe-deposit vault at the bank, the locksmith will use a drill with a hardened steel tip to drill out the core of the lock—at your considerable expense.)

The pin tumbler lock became enormously popular. Although it was not completely pickproof, it was highly secure and relatively easy and inexpensive to make.

Most of the early pin tumbler locks had four or five pins. The line dividing each pin could be placed low, high, or in between. This meant that with multiple pins, each cut in a different place, the lockmaker could produce thousands of locks and never have two that opened with the same key. The more pins in the lock, the more difficult it would be to pick, and the better the odds that no two people would have a key that

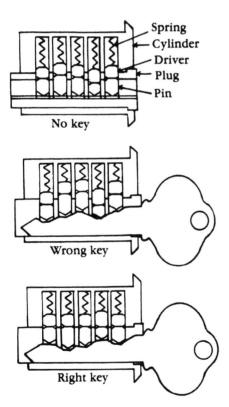

FIGURE 17. A modern pin tumbler lock. Springs force the pins into the center plug, preventing the lock from turning. A wrong key fails to align the break in the pins with the shear line, but the right key creates a shear line so the lock can turn. *Reprinted by permission of TAB Books from* Professional Locksmithing Techniques *by Bill Phillips. Copyright © 1991 by TAB Books, Inc.*

FIGURE 18. Two modern Yale locks guard the doors of a United States Post Office building. Note that Yale still uses a zigzag keyway.

fit the same lock. In theory there was no limit to the number of pins you could put in a lock. The famous Charles Hobbs estimated that a Yale pin lock could be created with as many as *forty* different pins. This lock and its key would be quite long—it might require a five-inch-thick door for installation—but it would certainly be unpickable, even for a Charles Hobbs.

Although there have been many improvements since the days of Linus Yale, Sr. and Jr., the pin tumbler lock is pretty much the standard for pick-resistant locks today. The chances are that the key to your front door fits a pin tumbler lock very similar to the locks that were invented and patented one hundred fifty years ago.

3

Safe and Secure

What is a "good" lock? Obviously, one that keeps the burglars out or your property locked safely.

But as we've seen, it is very difficult to make a perfect lock, one that can't be picked or broken. In fact James Edgar and William McInerny state flatly that "no lock is completely invulnerable to attack." They add that the real quality of a lock depends on how well it slows down or inconveniences a thief:

> An expert can pick an average pin tumbler lock in a matter of seconds, and no lock can survive strong force applied for a sufficient length of time. The sole object of using any lock at all is to *delay* an intruder. A good lock makes entry riskier and more trouble than it's worth, and that is the objective.

There are all kinds of ways a lock can be compromised—broken into or gotten around. Lost keys may be found by a stranger who may figure out what they open. A boss can give a set of keys to an employee who loses or misuses them. Locks can be picked or simply broken or sawed off or filed open.

37

Two stories of burglary and breaking and entering illustrate the problems.

In 1865 a London jeweler named Walker put some especially prized gems in his safe and locked it tightly. Before locking the doors to his shop, he placed iron shutters on the windows to keep thieves from breaking the glass and entering his shop that way. He left small slits in the shutters so police could peer in during their patrols, and he arranged mirrors to show police the hidden corners of the room. Even if a thief managed to get in, he would likely be spotted by the British police officer, or bobby.

Over the weekend thieves broke into the second floor rooms, cut a hole in the floor, and dropped into a tailor shop next door to Walker's. They tried to cut through the wall into the jewelry shop but—ah-ha—Walker had built the wall of metal plate, which the burglars couldn't penetrate. The tireless burglars cut through to the basement of the tailor shop, moved their equipment under the jewelry shop, and cut a hole up through the floor. They now had all weekend to work; whenever a bobby came around, they would drop back into the basement so the jewelry shop appeared to be empty. But they weren't home free yet, because they encountered a safe that had been designed as thief proof. They weren't able to pick the lock. Instead they used wedges to spring the door off its hinges. Despite Walker's careful preparations, he lost the jewelry.

As Edgar and McInerny have said, given enough time, lockcrackers can figure out a way to get into or past any lock.

Or take the security of the Folkestone train, which ran from London to Paris. Valuable shipments were placed in a lockbox for which there were only two keys. One key was given to the owner who was shipping valuable property; the other was in the possession of the superintendent of traffic in Folkestone, where the train would be loaded on a ferryboat and shipped across the English channel.

On May 15, 1885, gold valued at twelve thousand British pounds was stolen from the Folkestone night train. Nobody could figure out how it was done. The gold had been placed in the strongbox; the box had been locked and weighed. The box had been weighed again in Bologne, on the French side of the English channel, and its weight was the same, indicating that the gold was still there. However, when the box was opened in Paris, it was found to contain lead pellets. The bullion itself had vanished somewhere along the way.

Detectives were not able to solve the crime. But sixteen months later, one of the criminals confessed. It seems he had been caught writing bad checks, and he told about the Folkestone caper in the hope of getting a light sentence.

The thieves had planned very carefully. To learn about the security system, the thieves had, months earlier, actually made a shipment by the Folkestone night train. As they went through the process, they carefully observed all security procedures, and most important, where the keys were kept. Later, on a particularly busy day at Folkestone, they were able to make an impression of the master key while the superintendent had his back turned. With an illegal key in their possession, it was fairly easy for them to break into the secure train car after the train left London, remove the gold, replace it with lead, and leave the train with the gold as it arrived in Folkestone. Once again a lock hadn't failed, but the security system had.

Even after the development of the pin tumbler lock in the middle 1900s, lockmakers and lockpicks continued their wars. Thieves used gunpowder, acid, and diamond drills to break locks or get into safes and strongboxes. Lockmakers responded with the use of stronger steel and drillproof (or drill *resistant*) locks. Manufacturers beefed up the strength of doors and hinges in their strongboxes. Lockmakers put more and more pins into their locks, increasing the complexity of picking.

The Yale family, for example, created a series of what they called infallible bank locks. (See Figure 19.) One of their creations, the Double Infallible, had two keys for an eight-tumbler lock, whose key pattern could be changed. The whole lock had over one hundred moving parts and weighed forty-six pounds. Other Yale bank locks were called the Yale Magic Bank Lock, the Double Treasury Bank Lock, and the Monitor Bank Lock.

FIGURE 19. A Yale infallible lock. *Smithsonian Institution*

The Keyless Combination

An important development at this time was the creation of combination
locks, which work without keys. The idea of the combination lock was
not new; many locks in the Middle Ages had been designed to open if
the user set a series of dials in the proper order. The newer locks, however,
were more difficult to open. Basically, a modern combination lock works
with a series of inner dials. When the user spins to the outer dial numbers
in the proper sequence, gaps in the inner dials line up to form a gate,
allowing a bolt to move. In many ways a good combination lock is more
secure than a keyed lock because there is no keyhole for a lockpick to
penetrate. Also, a combination lock has so many possible number se-

quences that it is quite unlikely a thief can come up with the right one in a short time.

For example a Eureka lock patented by the Dodds, MacNeal, & Urban Company in 1862 had 1,073,741,824 possible combinations; the company estimated that it would require 2,042 years, 324 days, and 1 hour for a thief to try them all. (That would certainly slow down the thief, although there is the possibility that he or she might hit the right combination on the very first try.)

Sometimes on television you'll see a burglar spinning the dial of a combination lock, listening carefully with his or her ear to the dial, and presto, the safe opens. Sometimes these TV safecrackers will sandpaper their fingertips to get a good feel for a lock. There is both truth and myth to these images. James Edgar and William McInerny report that until about fifty years ago, it was possible to crack some combination locks by listening to a faint sound when tumblers fell into place. Or a skilled safecracker could feel the friction of the tumblers and line up the gates by touch. But today, Edgar and McInerny add, "Tumblers in combination locks do not 'click,' despite Hollywood's contentions to the contrary." Newer locks contain sound-muffling devices, silent plastic mechanisms, and other devices that quiet the sound of the lock. At one time, X rays could be used to discover the pattern of tumblers, but that technique too has been thwarted by the use of plastic materials that don't show up on X-ray screens.

Underwriter's Laboratory, which tests out locks and rates their strength, requires that a modern high-quality combination lock resist entry for at least twenty man-hours, long enough to discourage any thief who doesn't have a whole weekend to spend on the job.

Safes and Security

Edwin Holmes, the man who is generally credited with being the first to invent a successful burglar alarm, once wrote, "The whole history of bank burglary and vault building is competitive." There is competition within the industry for better designs and competition between the lock companies and the lockpicks out there on the street.

One hundred years ago, the refinement of combination locks solved some security problems for banks and jewelers. Still, safecracking remained possible. Thus lockmakers and safe builders began using a variety of techniques and strategies to make it difficult to gain access.

James Sargent, a New York lockmaker, was the first to think of rigging a clock to a bank vault. Even if one picked the lock or unscrambled the combination, the bolt of the vault could not be opened until a certain

FIGURE 20. A Mosler double-door safe. *Mosler, Inc.*

FIGURE 21. A train carrying the world's largest safe from Ohio to San Francisco, 1875. *Diebold, Inc.*

time. As a precaution against clock failure, Sargent even put two clocks in his vault devices.

Two Ohio companies—Mosler and Diebold—helped to make Cincinnati "The Safe Capital of the World." The Mosler Company developed a screw-door burglary safe with three separate time locks, and its engineers eliminated any holes or openings in the dial where a criminal might push explosives or corrosive chemicals. Mosler created double-door safes (see Figure 20), twice the trouble for safecrackers, and the company experimented with drillproof and torchproof materials.

Both Diebold and Mosler boasted about the fireproof capabilities of their equipment as well, and both had safes that survived the famous Chicago fire of 1870 and were opened later to reveal undamaged contents. Diebold happily reported that 878 of their safes had survived, preserving the contents successfully. Diebold also manufactured larger and larger vaults, and in 1875 set a world record, building a vault so large it required a forty-seven-car train (see Figure 21) to haul it to its final resting place at the San Francisco Safe Deposit Company.

An article appearing in the *New York Times* in 1894 told just how tough Mosler safes and locks had become:

> There was a blockade at Broadway and Leonard Street yesterday morning that delayed traffic for several hours. Men jostled and crowded one another to get to the middle of the throng and see what was being so curiously watched. Those who succeeded in pushing their way through the dense gathering found the innocent cause of all the excitement to be a man engaged in deliberately "cracking" a safe that had been hauled out of the ruins of the fire that gutted this corner. . . .

The safe had actually been on the third floor of the building, but as the floors burned, it had plunged to the basement, where the fire was hottest. It was hauled out, and the "cracksman" worked for several hours with hammer and chisel:

> At last a shout went up as the safe doors were forced open. The owner and his clerks, who had been waiting patiently all the time to see if the money, books, and other valuables remained intact after the thorough roasting the safe had received, came forward and began to remove them. To their delight they found everything intact. The contents were neither burned nor injured by water.

Years later, safe companies were still testing out new materials and boasting about the strength of their products. During World War I (1914–1918) the Mosler Company used its knowledge of tough metals to build tank treads (see Figure 22) and then explained that the same metals were used in its Quadruple Manganese Steel Bank Safe, "The Most Indestructible Thing Man Has Ever Made."

Mosler too had testimonials from people who had tried to break into their safes. Willie Sutton, a famous safecracker, wrote in his autobiography (from jail) that once when he was breaking into a jewelry store, "My heart sank when I saw it was a Mosler safe. Those Mosler people certainly make safe safes." A California burglar broke into a department store and spent half the night trying to crack the safe. When he failed

FIGURE 22. An advertisement for safes and tank treads made by Mosler, Inc. *Mosler, Inc.*

he typed a note to the store manager congratulating him on having purchased an uncrackable safe.

Nowadays, vaults are very strong indeed. The Bank Protection Act requires that banks be equipped with tamper resistant door and window locks, and that the vaults be constructed with twelve-inch-thick reinforced concrete walls, floors, and ceilings. The vault door must be three-and-a-half inches thick, and it must be both drill and torch resistant. Usually a bank vault will be equipped with a dial lock and a time lock, plus a lockable gate to keep out unauthorized people when the bank is open for business. The electrical supply to the vault will be run through pipes or conduits one-and-a-half inches thick, and these will be designed so as not to provide a direct path to the vault, preventing burglars from running long tubes or cables or tools in through the wiring. Bank vaults are also equipped with ventilators in case a person gets locked in, but these too must be designed in ways not to allow access from the outside.

Bank vaults have gotten so tough that it is rare to find thieves attacking one directly. Although in the 1990s bank robberies are on the increase in the United States, most often the thieves bypass the main vault. They prefer to stick up tellers in the bank itself or, even more commonly, to rob people as they leave a bank or an automatic teller, or money machine. There's an expression in the burglary business: "If the bank safe is too tough to crack, kidnap the bank president for ransom." With modern safes and vaults, kidnapping may be easier for a criminal than trying to crack the bank. (Neither safecracking nor kidnapping is recommended as a career option for readers of this book.)

Lockpicks and Their Tools

For everyday lockups, most of us don't have the luxury of reinforced concrete walls and torch proof steel doors. Most people continue to rely on keys and locks much like those first developed by Linus Yale. A key inserted in a lock raises spring-loaded pins just the right amount, allowing an inner cylinder, or plug, to turn, rotating a bolt. (To remind yourself of how these pin tumbler locks work, refer back to Figure 17, page 35.) And pin tumbler locks *can* be picked.

On television you'll often see the bad guys or the detective hero pick a lock in nothing flat. Somebody slides a credit card in the doorway or pushes an unkinked paper clip in the lock and it's "Open Sesame."

In real life lockpicking is not so easy. To get a quality rating from Underwriter's Laboratory, a pin tumbler lock must resist picking for at least six minutes. (Imagine how boring TV would be if you actually had to watch somebody spend six minutes picking a lock.)

The easiest kind of lock to pick is one commonly found in the home, a door lock with a spring latch that automatically locks the door as you leave the house. Here a thin card, or shim, can be inserted between the door and the doorsill to push back the latch. Often this is done with a credit card, and the process is called " 'loiding," from cellu*loid*, a kind of plastic. This is the technique you most often see on TV. However, in most real-life doors, access to the latch is blocked by a strip of wood or metal, so that you can only get at the latch by taking off the protective barriers.

(Warning to Readers: "Don't try 'loiding or any of the other lockpicking techniques I will describe in this chapter. You will probably wind up doing damage to a lock, door, or sill if you experiment with lockpicking techniques. Most locksmiths know these strategies, but they are licensed and bonded to make certain they do not misuse their skills. Some states will not allow locksmithing, including lockpicking, to be taught to young people under the age of eighteen.)

The other major method of lockpicking involves penetrating the lock itself. Two different kinds of tools are required: a torsion (or tension) wrench and a pick. A torsion wrench is a thin bar with a small bend or hook on the end, rather like the tool the dentist uses to scrape your teeth, but smaller. It is used to place pressure on the center plug of the lock, as if you put your key in a lock and just barely started to turn it. The pick itself is a thin tool designed to fit the keyway. The locksmith wiggles the tool, and by feel and experience, raises the pins, one by one, to the shear line. When a pin is raised to the right level and one can feel a little

play in the lock, the torsion wrench wedges the pin at the right height—
its open position. The locksmith raises the pins, one by one, and wedges
them into place until all pins have reached the shear line and the lock
will turn. Because keyways, keyholes, and pin systems differ from one
lock to another, a locksmith or burglar will carry several different shapes
of picks and torsion wrenches. (See Figure 23.)

Sometimes a lockpick will use a shortcut method called "raking" a
lock. Here, a zigzag piece of wire is inserted in the lock and sawed gently
back and forth. The zigs and zags in the wire will raise the pins to different
heights and, by chance, most of them will sooner or later be at the shear
line. By keeping pressure on the lock at the same time, the lockpick will
lodge each pin at the right height and the lock will open.

There is even an electric version of a rake called a lock gun. Its tip is
inserted in the lock and vibrated by a tiny electric motor. Like raking a
lock this vibration jiggles the pins, causing them to move up and down,
by chance being wedged at the shear line with pressure from a torsion
wrench.

A cruder method of opening a pin tumbler lock is called "rapping."
With a torsion wrench in place, the lockpick gives a hard rap, or knock,
on the door, causing the pins to jump up and be snagged at the right
level. Again, *don't try this yourself,* because you will likely just damage
the lock.

There are other methods of opening a pin lock as well. In "impressioning," the lockpick inserts something into the lock such as a blank or
uncut key or a piece of soft metal. Using a pair of pliers or a similar tool,
the person pushes upward on the blank to get a marking of where the
pins fall. Impressioning can also be done with a blank key that has been
"sooted," or smoked in a match flame. When inserted in the lock and
wiggled, the key shows bright metal at the points where the pins make
contact. No matter how the impression is obtained, the next step is to
use small files, a blank or uncut key, and some trial and error. The person
files down a blank key, tests it, files some more, until a key that fits has
been created.

For a burglar a modern-day lock presents many difficulties. Most se-

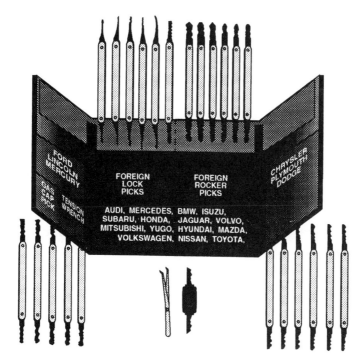

FIGURE 23. Professional lockpicking tools for automobiles. *Lock Technology, Inc., Naperville, Illinois*

rious lockpicking is done by licensed and registered locksmiths, who are called on to open a place that has been locked by accident or to which the keys have been lost. The owner doesn't want doors and windows damaged and thus calls a locksmith.

Burglars, on the other hand, are looking for the easiest and fastest way in. New York City detective Guy Capolupo describes burglary as "a crime of opportunity," in which the burglar looks for places that are quick and easy to enter and exit. "The average burglar doesn't know much—but he knows more—about doors and locks than the average tenant," says Detective Capolupo. Often the thief knows that the door or the hinges are weaker than the lock and will use a crowbar or screwdriver to pop open the door, rather than try the slow process of picking a lock. Some doors are hollow core, made from thin sheets of wood, and these are easily broken. Often back entrance doors in houses contain glass, allowing a burglar to break the window and reach in to twist the knob from the inside. And windows and sliding glass doors are generally opened easily with tools as simple as a screwdriver or an ordinary knife from the dining table.

Stray Keys and the Security Problem

A major problem with keys is that they get lost or that you don't have the one you need when you need it. If you lose your keys, there is the danger that thieves will find them and figure out what door they fit. (For example a stolen purse will often contain the owner's address as well as a set of keys.)

It is a tradition, too, for people to keep an extra key outside their house in case they lose their keys and are locked out. They may leave an extra key under the doormat, over the doorsill, or taped to the bottom of the mailbox. Such hiding places are so common that thieves will often look there first and find the key.

A bit more clever is a device called a Key Stone, something you can buy at novelty gift shops. It is a fake stone cast from rocklike material, with a hollow chamber for hiding a key. You insert the key in the chamber and toss this stone in your front yard, under the bushes, or any likely place where a rock might come to rest. The burglar is presumably fooled by this trick. However, you have to wonder whether, knowing of these devices, a burglar might also check any unusual stones in the vicinity of your front door.

More secure is a device called the Supra Key Safe, actually a small safe with a combination lock mounted near or on your door (see Figure 24). You can give friends the combination to get at the regular key, while a burglar would still have to go to the considerable difficulty of picking a combination lock. This device is widely used by real estate agents who want to show a house while the owner is away. Local, trustworthy agents are given the combination and thus can get into the house whenever they need to.

On a much larger scale, the Knox Company has a system that can be imagined as a gigantic key-under-the-mat plan, only a secure one. Imag-

FIGURE 24. A Supra Key minisafe hangs on a door. It contains a key to the front door.

ine you are a fire department called to a burning office building. You and your crew need to get into the building, but the front door is locked. Even if you break down the front door, you will find every office in the place locked, making it almost impossible for you to fight the blaze. The Knox Box (see Figure 25) is a high security storage vault that is located outside the building. It contains a key to every door in the building. A key to the Knox Box itself is stored at the fire department. In case of an emergency, the fire department can open the Knox Box, find the right keys, and get in.

Yet another way of assuring that the right people can get past the right

FIGURE 25. A Knox Box for key storage. The fire fighter has a key to the safe box, which contains all the keys to a building. *The Knox Company*

locks at the right time is through a system known as "master keying." Under this plan, one key, the master key, will open every door in a building. Other keys known as submasters will open sets of doors, say, all the doors on the second floor. Still other keys will work with only one of the locks in the building. To accomplish this, master keyed locks contain pins made up of two or more smaller pins. (See Figure 26.) All locks in the building have a set of pins that the master key will raise to the right height, allowing the lock to turn. The submasters have a different set of pins that can be opened by the master and the submaster keys, and the individual lock has a set that can be opened by the individual key, possibly by a submaster, and by the master key.

Designing a master key system is obviously quite complicated. A German company, Lips' Safe and Lock Manufacturing Company, once designed an unusually elaborate system for use on an ocean liner. The ship

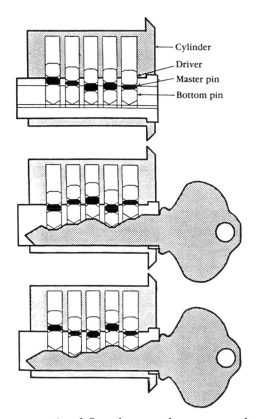

FIGURE 26. A master key. The dark "master pins" create different shear lines so that more than one key can open the lock. *Reprinted by permission of TAB Books from* Professional Locksmithing Techniques *by Bill Phillips. Copyright © 1991 by TAB Books, Inc.*

contained five thousand rooms, each with a lock. For passenger security each lock had to be different. However, the captain of the ship would need to have a master key that would open all five thousand locks, giving him access to any cabin. On each of the ten ship decks, a steward would have a submaster key that would open all the locks on his deck, about five hundred locks altogether. In addition, because of concerns for passenger safety and health, the system included a special key for the ship's doctor that would allow him to open passenger doors, even if they were bolted from the inside. Thus if a person became ill and could not unbolt the door, the doctor could get in anyway. The captain, on the other hand, could not enter rooms when people were in them, since the passengers would want to protect their privacy in their own rooms. Moreover, the system included provision for the doctor to be locked *out* of the rooms when the door was *not* bolted from the inside, assuring passengers that the doctor would not be going into their rooms without authority. Although the system was complicated, the Lips' Company did design the master key successfully.

There is another interesting problem associated with master locks. Imagine that you are in charge of a security system for an apartment building. When a tenant moves out, you have to change the locks on the apartment to protect the security of the new tenant. Changing locks—or rekeying, as it is called—is expensive, especially if you are part of a master key system. A company named InstaKey has developed a system whereby a number of tiny wafers are inserted in the pin cavity of a lock. Using a special key, the building superintendent can dislodge and pull out one of the wafers, which changes the key pattern for the lock while keeping the lock a part of the master key system. In this way, the lock can be changed in less than a minute, giving the new tenant security while preserving the master key system.

High Security Locks

As you will see in chapter 6, some of the security problems with lock-picking can be solved with electronic lock systems. In fact, some experts predict that during your lifetime, metal keys and mechanical locks will become obsolete, replaced by other methods of gaining entry. But for the present, mechanical locks and keys are in use by the millions, if not billions. There is no inexpensive electronic substitute for a portable padlock, for example, and in contrast to many electronic systems, good old-fashioned locks and keys are inexpensive.

In fact many manufacturers continue to make improvements on the basic pin tumbler lock as invented by the Egyptians and refined by the Yale family. The quest for an unpickable lock continues.

For example the Kaba Company makes a super-high security lock that involves not one set of pins but three, set at angles to one another. There can be up to sixteen pins per lock (making the lock much less pickable than a five- or six-pin lock), including "mushroom bottom" pins that resist being manipulated by a lockpicking tool. The whole system is designed to be drill resistant, impression resistant, and pick resistant.

The Dom Company makes a lock that is especially burglar resistant. (See Figure 27.) The key to a Dom lock has dimples on the flat side of the key rather than zigzag cuts in the key itself. *Two* rows of pins (rather than the usual *one*) are lined up inside the lock cylinder. When the Dom key enters the lock, each pin drops into a dimple on the key, creating a shear line and allowing the lock to open.

Other lock companies have developed equally interesting designs for harder-than-ever-to-pick locks. There are hollow, round keys to fit circular keyways; combinations of wards (remember the warded locks of the Middle Ages?) that make entry and picking difficult; six-sided keys for twelve-pin locks; pins that jam in the lock if not opened with a proper key; keys whose ragged edges are cut at angles rather than straight across; and push-button systems that get away from the use of keys altogether. It's safe to assume that as long as mechanical locks continue to be needed, manufacturers will seek ways to improve them and to keep us safe and secure.

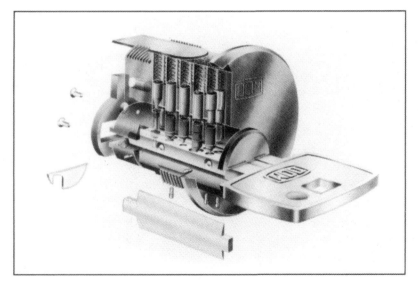

FIGURE 27. Dom high security lock with dimpled key and two rows of pins. *Black & Decker Canada, Ltd.*

4 Legendary Locks and Keys

Most of the locks and keys built over the centuries have served their purpose quietly, without drawing attention to themselves. They open and shut for years and years, and eventually they wear out or break or are lost and forgotten.

However, some locks and keys are unique because of how they function or how they are constructed or simply because of their size, large or small. In this chapter we'll look at some locks and keys that have stood the test of time and are re-membered in history.

Khufu's Tomb

Imagine a lock that measures 755 feet (about two-and-a-half football fields) along each of four sides and rises 481 feet tall (four plus basketball courts end-to-end). A lock that covers thirteen acres of land. A lock that was built from 2.3 million blocks of stone, each weighing between two and fifteen tons. A lock that required one hundred thousand workers and took twenty years to complete.

This is the Great Pyramid of Giza, in Egypt, built as a tomb for the ruler Khufu. Now, the Great Pyramid is not a lock in the usual sense, and it doesn't resemble the wooden pin locks used by Egyptian locksmiths over five thousand years ago. But like a lock, it was designed to protect something valuable, in this case the body of the king himself, along with tons of gold, jewels, household valuables, and family papers.

The Egyptian rulers wanted to make certain their bodies and their treasures would be protected after death so they could go into the afterlife in their accustomed style. The treasures would supply them with money to use in the world beyond, and the pyramids were created to keep the ruler protected from vandals or others who might steal the treasure or desecrate the body.

The pyramids were constructed with complicated inner chambers and corridors. The actual chamber where the body of Khufu was laid to rest is toward the very center of the Great Pyramid. Nearby was a chamber for the body of his queen. After the mummified corpses had been placed in their chambers, the passageways were sealed off, and the workers escaped from the pyramid by way of secret exit corridors. In some Egyptian pyramids false chambers were constructed containing the body of someone about the ruler's size, thus attempting to trick grave robbers. Special chapels were also built inside the pyramids so family members could pay respects to the dead.

So, how did this gigantic lock work?

Not so well. When archaeologists were able to get into the Great Pyramid in modern times, they discovered it had been burglarized, and most of the evidence suggests that the robbery took place soon after the death of Khufu.

The Maze of the Minotaur

Greek mythology tells us of another sort of lock, a maze that housed the feared Minotaur, a creature with the body of a man and the head of a bull. The favorite food of the Minotaur was people: human sacrifices. A complex maze, or labyrinth, was constructed by Daedalus (the man who also invented wings for himself and his son, Icarus). In the center of the maze lived the Minotaur. The maze presumably kept the Minotaur locked up, but it also made it impossible for human sacrifices to escape as well. Sooner or later, people would make a wrong turn and wind up face-to-face with the Big M.

In those days King Minos of the island of Crete had conquered the people of Athens. As a yearly tribute he demanded seven maidens and seven young men. These young people were turned loose in the maze, and because they couldn't find their way out, they were eventually devoured by the Minotaur.

One brave Athenian, Theseus, decided to bring an end to this slaughter. He volunteered to be one of the sacrifices and was taken to Crete. There he met and fell in love with the king's daughter, Ariadne. Not wanting to see her lover killed, Ariadne gave Theseus two things: a magic sword and a skein of thread. Entering the maze, Theseus unwound the thread, leaving a trail behind him. After slaying the Minotaur with the magic sword, he opened the lock of the maze by following the string safely back to the opening, bringing his thirteen companions with him.

Scylla and Charybdis

Greek mythology also tells of a different sort of lock that protected the Strait of Messina, between the foot of the Italian boot and the island of Sicily. Scylla was (and still is) a sharp, rocky point of land on which many ships have crashed. To the Greeks, Scylla became a monster with twelve feet, six necks, and six mouths, each with three rows of gnashing teeth. In paintings Scylla wears a belt of dogs' heads around her waist.

Charybdis is actually a whirlpool near the Messina, but in the mythic imagination it became a monster sucking in and belching out water, boats, and anything else that came near it. In the Greek story *The Odyssey,* the sailors have to navigate a careful course between Scylla and Charybdis to avoid being attacked by either one. The hero Odysseus successfully unlocks the passage by sailing skillfully, but not before losing six men to the teeth of Scylla.

Another Greek lock that protected a waterway were the Symplegades, two giant rocks at the entrance to the Black Sea. The story is told that these two rocks would crash together whenever a boat went between them, crushing the boat and its occupants. In one myth, Jason and the crew of his ship, *Argo,* are on a quest to find a golden fleece, the wool of a magic sheep. They must pass through the Symplegades to pursue their quest. Jason cleverly releases a bird to fly between the rocks, which smash together, just missing the bird and pulling out one of its tail feathers. While the rocks are backing off, preparing for another charge, Jason and his men power through the opening safely.

The Gordian Knot

We saw in chapter 1 that knots have served as locks. A complicated knot could slow down a burglar, and if it were improperly retied, it would serve as a warning that someone had been tampering. The most famous of these knots was tied by Gordius of Phyrgia, who hailed from a land near the eastern end of the Mediterranean Sea. Born a peasant, Gordius fulfilled a prophecy that a man would appear at a certain time driving an ox cart. Gordius became king and left his ox cart as a kind of monument in a public square, tying the bow of his wagon with a complicated knot. A legend developed that whoever was able to untie the knot would become the ruler of all Asia. When Alexander the Great came to this place, he observed the knot. Some stories say that Alexander was able to unravel the knot successfully. A more popular story is that Alexander became frustrated by the knot and "untied" it with a powerful slash of his sword. Either way Alexander went on to become ruler of Asia, fulfilling the prophecy. Today the Gordian Knot symbolizes a knotty problem that somebody solves, or unlocks, by unusual or dramatic methods.

The Trojan Horse

As you may recall from mythology, a great war was once fought between the Trojans and the Greeks over Helen, wife of a Greek king, who was kidnapped by the Trojans. After years of fruitless battle, the Greeks were about to give up their siege of the walled city of Troy. Odysseus, however, had one final idea. The Greeks constructed a huge wooden horse and left it outside the city walls. Inside the belly of the horse was a secret compartment containing a number of Greek soldiers. Having left the horse in plain view of the walls of Troy, the remainder of the Greek army headed for home—or, at least, withdrew from sight. After a debate, the Trojans unlocked and opened the city gates, brought in the horse, and locked the gates behind it. That night, the Greeks in the belly of the horse came out of hiding, unlocked the city gates from the inside, and let in the rest of the Greek army, which had not retreated from the scene after all. If the tomb of Khufu is the world's largest lock, the Trojan Horse may have been the world's largest key.

The Kicking, Counting Lock

In chapter 2 we saw how complicated locks became during the Middle Ages. Although the locks were not particularly secure by modern standards, locksmiths developed interesting ways to conceal the mechanism and guard against improper entry. One of the most elaborate and famous of these was a lock crafted by Johannes Wilkes of Birmingham, England. The lock was created in the shape of a man dressed in hunting clothes. On the lock was etched a poem, supposedly spoken by the hunter:

> If I had ye [your] gift of tongue
> I would declare and do no wrong
> Who ye ar yt [that] come by stealth
> to impare my Masters welth.

To open the lock, one first had to know to lift the hat on this silent watchman. Lifting the hat freed a mechanism that allowed one of the man's legs to be raised in a kicking action, thus revealing the keyhole. The man's finger pointed at a dial on the lock, and every time the key was turned, the finger pointed at the next higher number. Thus this was a detector lock that could tell its owner whether or not it had been opened in his absence. Without speaking a word, the kicking hunter could convey a great deal of information.

Catherine the Great's Necklace

The empress of Russia, ruling from 1762 to 1796, was deeply interested in locks. One lock believed to be from the collection of Catherine the Great is shown in Figure 13 (page 22). The Schlage Antique Lock Museum in San Francisco has another of Catherine's locks that itself tells a fascinating story.

A Russian lockmaker had been imprisoned in Siberia, thousands of miles from the Russian capital of Saint Petersburg. He heard about the interest of the empress in locks and started making a necklace of tiny locks and keys. He finally forged a total of eighty-nine padlocks and keys, each about half the size of a pinky fingernail. Each one of the locks actually worked. These were strung together into a necklace, and Catherine was so delighted that she let the man go free. There is now a Russian proverb based on this story: "It takes eighty-nine keys to unlock a prison."

King Louis the Lockmaker

Another ruler who was interested in locks was King Louis XVI of France, husband of the famous Marie Antoinette. Louis actually made locks as a hobby and was extremely proud of a cabinet he had created, complete with locked places for hiding papers. During the French Revolution, rebel leaders were able to break into the cabinet and read the papers. In part because of evidence against him found in the papers, he was declared guilty of crimes against the state and beheaded by the guillotine. It was said of him that "he was no better a locksmith than he was a king."

The Speckled Band

A popular form of detective story is the "locked-room mystery." Usually a person is found dead—murdered—in a room that was locked from the inside. The question is: How was the murder committed and how did the murderer get out of the room?

One of the most famous and imaginative of these stories is a Sherlock Holmes mystery, "The Speckled Band," by Sir Arthur Conan Doyle. Servants of a retired military colonel hear a horrible scream in the night. They go to the colonel's room to find it locked, and they break in to find the colonel dead. No one else is in the room. There is no other door. The windows are tightly shuttered. There is an odd clue, however: One of the servants thought he saw a speckled band around the colonel's head, but there is no band to be found later. Sherlock Holmes is called in. After inspecting the room carefully, he determines to spend a night in the murder room to test out a theory. In the middle of the dark night he awakens and, with his walking stick, whacks a bell rope used by the colonel to call his servants.

Holmes then cries out for lights, and everybody rushes to an adjoining room, where they find another man, dying, with a speckled band around his head. The man is, in fact, the killer, and the speckled band is a poisonous snake that had been trained to crawl through a ventilator and down the bell rope to kill the colonel. Sherlock Holmes's thrashing with his stick had sent the snake back up the rope, where it attacked its master.

The key to the mystery, as Holmes explained, is that a room may be locked against humans, but that doesn't mean that other things can't get in and out. Most locked-room mysteries work in a similar way, with the killer figuring out how to do his or her work from outside the locked room, say by blowing poison gas through the keyhole. Another popular (but less clever) solution is to have a secret panel through which the killer escapes. Sometimes the killer will rig up a string system that allows him or her to flip the lock from outside the room after the killing has been done. The point of all this is to make it appear that the victim died of natural causes or committed suicide, thus allowing the killer to go free.

Fort Knox

Fort Knox, Kentucky, is one of the most famous lockups in the world. Since 1937 it has been the depository, or home, of much of the gold supply of the United States. As you probably know, paper money in itself is worth, well, the paper it is printed on—not very much. It gains its value when the country that issues it has valuables, usually gold and silver, held in reserve to back it up. As a strong world currency, the United States dollar has always had solid gold reserves.

The vault system at Fort Knox was developed by the Mosler Company of Cincinnati. The doors were built twenty-one inches thick from the toughest, most torch resistant steel then known. The door alone weighed twenty tons, and the whole vault was encased in concrete walls about twenty-five inches thick. A newspaper at the time reported that

> . . . one series of shipments brought $5,500,000,000 worth of gold to Ft. Knox under the heaviest guard imaginable. Machine gunners, armed motorcycle riders, treasury agents and scores of soldiers escorted the treasure to its new home. Eventually, about half of the Nation's $20,400,000,000 worth of gold—about 80 per cent of the World's monetary gold—will be stored in this "impregnable fortress."

In fact Fort Knox is so heavily guarded that it would be impossible even to get near the vault. When I telephoned Fort Knox for information for this book, the officer at the fort told me all details about the vaults at Fort Knox are "classified information." We don't know exactly how much gold is stored there today, but since gold prices have risen enormously since 1937, we can guess that it is at least ten to twenty times the value of fifty years ago.

One popular movie proposed a fanciful way of getting at the Fort Knox treasury. In a James Bond thriller the archcriminal Goldfinger decides to corner the gold market and thus rule (and ruin) the world's economy. He realizes that it would be very difficult to haul all that gold away from Fort Knox, even if he could crack the security system. So he figures out a way to steal the gold without actually having to remove it from the vault. Gassing the Fort Knox soldiers-guards into unconsciousness, he plants an atomic bomb in the vault. James Bond, the hero, happens to be handcuffed to the bomb, which has a detonation timer. Goldfinger's idea is that when the bomb goes off (taking with it the pesky Agent 007), the gold in Fort Knox will become radioactive and thus valueless. This, in turn, will increase the value of Goldfinger's holdings and leave him on top of the economy. But James Bond manages to dismantle the timing device with just seconds to spare.

Curses. Gold foiled again!

The Coca-Cola Formula

The Coca-Cola Company has always carefully guarded its secret recipe for the flavoring of a Coke. The original mixture was created by John S. Pemberton, an Atlanta, Georgia, pharmacist. Experimenting with medicine recipes, he combined extracts from the leaves of the coca plant and the seeds of the cola tree. The syrup was mixed with carbonated water and became so popular that Dr. Pemberton eventually sold the formula to a businessman, Asa Candler, who carefully guarded the secret. The formula was kept in a fireproof safe, locked with a combination known only to Mr. Candler and his trusted associate Frank Robinson. Mr. Candler and Mr. Robinson would write out all the purchase orders themselves, so that nobody could figure out the formula. When ingredients arrived, the labels were peeled off the containers, which were stacked in a locked room where only trusted employees were allowed. Even then, few people knew what was in the containers. Workers making the syrup would have to memorize the locations of containers on the shelves and concoct the recipe not really knowing what ingredients they were using.

When it came time for Asa Candler to retire, he called his son, Howard, to him and passed on the formula. Howard Candler later wrote, "The total number of persons who have known the secret formula since Dr. Pemberton's day can be added up on the fingers of one hand."

Competitors have even taken the Coca-Cola Company to court to get it to unlock the secret of its special flavor. In a famous trial in 1917 the company had to demonstrate that Coke was a unique product in order to protect its patents. But even then the Coca-Cola Company was able to say only that "essential oils" and "plant extractives" were present, which didn't tell much to the competitors.

The traditional recipe for Coca-Cola is still a carefully guarded secret. Phillip Mooney, the archivist and historian of the Coca-Cola Company, explains:

> Only a small number of people know the precise way in which all the ingredients combine to form the syrup that is the basis for the finished product. The Coca-Cola Company goes to great lengths to protect the security of the formula and to insure that it will remain a secret. The formula is maintained in a vault in the Trust Company of Georgia.

The Hope Diamond

Of course sometimes you *don't* want treasures to be locked out of sight. The Crown Jewels of England, for example, are something that people want to see, and they are on view in a carefully guarded display within the famous Tower of London. (See chapter 5 for one story of the Tower and its keys.)

In our own country a national treasure is the Hope Diamond, one of the world's most famous jewels, weighing in at 45.42 carats. Most diamonds in rings are less than 1 carat. A diamond of more than 1 carat attracts attention as "a real rock." The Hope Diamond is a Rock Plus, a superstar among diamonds, about the size of a fifty-cent piece. It is a popular display at the Museum of Natural History in Washington, D.C. To show the Hope Diamond, the Diebold Company created a vault with a large porthole, or window, of heavy, burglarproof glass. (See Figure 28.) The vault gives the diamond both visibility and protection. In fact most visitors to the exhibit don't even realize that they are peering into a vault.

"Heist" movies, where thieves figure out how to steal a carefully guarded jewel, are a popular genre. The *Pink Panther* movies, for example, started out with the theft of a famous diamond that seemed to have a tiny pink panther at its center.

Perhaps the most famous movie of that kind is *Topkapi*, where a huge "rock" is on display in a museum, protected not only by locked doors, but by a pressure-sensitive alarm system in the floor. If a person so much as steps on the floor when the system is on, alarms are sounded and

FIGURE 28. The Hope Diamond on display in its "porthole" safe. *Diebold Inc.*

special security doors fall, trapping the thief in the room, where the authorities will not deal kindly with him or her. The clever thieves in this movie look around for another, better way in, and find it through the roof of the museum. Entering through a skylight, they string ropes like trapeze artists and swing down to the jewel case. With a suction cup attached to a rope, they carefully raise the glass case and remove the diamond. The crooks escape with the jewel, but their crime is not perfect. As they leave the skylight, a bird flies in. Unknown to the thieves, the bird flies around the museum and eventually lands on the floor, setting off the alarm and leading to the capture of the would-be diamond thieves.

The Atomic Safe

After World War II and the development of the atomic bomb, the word *safe* took on new meaning. The incredible destructive force and heat generated by an atomic bomb was far more than any office safe or bank vault had experienced, whether through flood, fire, tornado, hurricane, or the use of acid or explosives. Lock and key manufacturers wondered just what would happen to safes in an atomic blast.

In 1955 the Mosler Company arranged to have some of its office safes taken to Yucca Flats, Nevada, where A-bombs were being tested. Safes were placed at varying distances from "ground zero," and the bomb was set off. Many of the safes survived the blast and protected their contents. However, Mr. Edwin Mosler, Jr., did say that "the closest ones [to ground zero] went around the World in a cloud of dust." Two years later, a large Mosler Company vault was also placed in the blast zone. Afterward it was discovered that the combination lock still worked successfully and that the temperature inside the vault had not increased. (See Figure 29.) Thus it was concluded that one could make a safe strong enough to survive nuclear attack. Of course in the event of a nuclear war, there might be nobody left to open that safe, and at the least, radioactivity would be so high that one wouldn't want to go into the blast zone anyway.

FIGURE 29. The Century Vault after an atomic blast. *Mosler, Inc.*

Preserving the Paper Trail

In the 1950s a cold war between Russia and the United States had everybody worrying about nuclear attack. Both sides exchanged threats and built up their stockpiles of nuclear weapons. Everybody hoped that the war would remain "cold" and not lead to an actual "hot" engagement.

Just in case, however, precautions were taken to protect important papers that are a part of our heritage. The United States National Archives in Washington, D.C., holds the original copies of several documents that are especially important in United States history: the Declaration of Independence, the United States Constitution, and the Bill of Rights. These are on display for interested visitors, but they are priceless and must be protected.

The security system is complex. Visitors to the archives must walk through a metal detector to make certain they do not have any tools or weapons that could be used to damage the documents. Two security guards stand beside the documents, which are enclosed in bronze-and-glass cases. Helium, an inert gas, is kept in the display cases to prevent decay from exposure to air, and the glass in the cases is tinted to filter out harmful light.

For our purposes the most interesting feature of the system is a massive Jack-in-the-Box vault, or safe, designed by the Mosler Company. (See Figure 30.) At night, or in the case of an emergency, the *entire exhibit* is lowered beneath the main floor of the archives building. The documents simply disappear from sight! Two steel arms, something like a pair of scissors or tongs, retract, lowering the documents, which gently drop about twenty-two feet into a vault below. Then massive doors on top of the vault swing shut. The vault weighs fifty-five tons and includes a chamber seven-and-a-half feet long, five feet wide, and six feet high. It even has its own power supply in case the electricity is cut off. At the dedication ceremony in 1952, President Harry S. Truman declared that this vault was "the safest safe man had ever devised."

Master's Bulletproof Padlock

For day-to-day living, most of us have a concern closer to home: We want our locks and padlocks to stand up to attack from people who would steal or damage our property. As we've seen, lockpicking is a sophisticated skill. Most burglars will try to break a lock open rather than pick it. A weak lock can often be damaged with a crowbar or heavy sledge hammer.

The Master Lock Company of Milwaukee has been in the lock business since 1921 and has long been concerned with the security of its products. The founder of the company, Harry Soref, experimented with laminated padlocks, where the case itself is built from many thin slices of steel. He reasoned that this sort of layered lock would protect the mechanism more adequately than a case shaped from sheets of metal. The company has been selling laminated padlocks ever since.

FIGURE 30. The mechanism of the Mosler Jack-in-the-Box safe that protects
United States documents. The smaller photo shows Vice-President Richard
Nixon and Senator John Bricker discussing a model of the vault with Edwin
Mosler, Jr. *Mosler, Inc.*

In 1964 Master launched a television advertising campaign showing a close-up of a Master lock being shot with the bullet from a .44 Magnum pistol. The lock didn't open. (See Figure 31.) Since then Master has repeated the experiment many times, with cameras running for its Tested-Tough commercials. In one set of trials a marksman plugged away at forty Master locks. Only one of the forty opened on the first shot. Thirty-three locks were shot a second time, and of those, only three opened. Master also reported that shots hitting the shackle, or U-bolt, of the lock merely ricocheted off the steel. (By the way, a good reason *not* to shoot at locks is the danger of a glancing bullet. Films that show people firing at a lock at close range are not only misleading but set a dangerous example. Shooting a lock is likely to lead to somebody getting hit with a stray bullet.)

FIGURE 31. A Master lock,
Tested Tough. *Master Lock Company*

The Watergate Burglary

This is the famous lock-and-key episode that led to the resignation of a president of the United States. On June 17, 1972, five men were caught breaking into the national headquarters of the Democratic party in Washington, D.C. The burglars had gotten through the security system at the Watergate office complex. The office building had a night clerk, and the distribution of keys to workers had been carefully controlled. A lock-picking specialist guesses that the burglars had made a key to a back entrance by impressioning, probably smoking a key blank with soot, inserting it in the lock, seeing where the soot had been worn away by the lock mechanism, and filing away until they had a key that fit. Other lock specialists suppose that the burglars used picking tools and torsion wrenches to get by the lock. Whatever technique they used to get in, they made a simple and foolish error: They placed a strip of duct tape over the latch mechanism to keep it open while they worked upstairs. A security guard found the door taped open and called the District of Columbia police, who easily caught the burglars.

Actually the burglars weren't stealing anything. Rather, they were in the process of installing electronic bugs—listening devices—in the Democratic headquarters. Nineteen seventy-two was an election year, and they wanted to listen in on campaign strategies so they could anticipate the moves of their opponents. In a long and complex investigation, it was revealed that members of the president's staff were aware of the planning of this burglary and that the president himself had some knowledge, if not of Watergate itself, at least of illicit practices being done by his staff. The public outrage was so great that Richard M. Nixon was forced to resign, the only president to resign in the history of the United States.

Kryptonite Bicycle Lock

Locking up a bicycle is almost a book chapter by itself. A bike is a large object, awkward to lock. A bike is also easily stolen, because a thief can simply hop on it and ride away. On the other hand, a bike lock has to be fairly light in weight; you don't want to ride around carrying twenty pounds of chain or a huge padlock.

Over the years numerous bike locks have been designed: Some bicycles come with built-in locks that prevent a bike from rolling (but such locks don't stop a thief from simply carrying off the bike). Some bikes have a handlebar lock that also keeps a thief from riding in anything but a straight line or a sharp curve (but, again, the thief can carry off the bike and pick the lock later).

Various kinds of chain and cable locks work more or less well, depending on their strength and the sophistication of their lock. However, serious thieves often carry around bolt or chain cutters that can snip through even heavy armored cable or all but the most expensive, case-hardened chains.

Enter Michael Zane, an inventor who came up with an idea that revolutionized the bicycle lock. Zane named his lock Kryptonite after the only material in the universe strong enough to kill Superman. A Kryptonite bike lock is about a foot long and looks like a horseshoe with a bar across the opening. (See Figure 32.) Made of a high density steel, it is covered with plastic to avoid scratching the bike. Tests have shown that it can't be opened by large bolt cutters and hacksaws and that it can't be whacked open with hammers or crowbars. Zane and the Kryptonite Company were so confident of their lock that they offered to buy the owner a new bicycle if one was stolen because of a lock failure.

In an impressive ad Kryptonite showed a bicycle that had been locked to a parking meter. The owner had removed the front wheel of the bike, looped the lock through the bike and wheel, then locked the whole thing to a parking meter. A thief came along and couldn't open the lock. Then, apparently, he or she tried to get at the bike by breaking off the parking meter itself. As the photo shows the thief did a great deal of damage to the concrete, but the bicycle remained safely locked.

What appeals to many bicyclists is the simplicity of the Kryptonite design. It can be carried in a bike bag or clipped to the frame of a bike; it weighs no more than a chain or cable lock that may be less secure and

FIGURE 32. A Kryptonite lock survives attack. *The Kryptonite Corporation*

more awkward to carry around. The lock has also received awards for its design: It has been on display at the Museum of Modern Art in New York City, the National Endowment for the Arts and Sciences in Washington, D.C., and the Museum of Practical Design in Germany. It has also received an award for good design in Japan. The Kryptonite lock, then, is legendary, not only because it works well, but because it looks good while doing so.

The List of Unusual Locks

There are far more legendary locks and keys than I can include in the chapter, so I'll close with a simple list of some of the more unusual locking devices that are around today. Many of these can be seen at the local locksmith or hardware store. Keep your eyes open for:

- spare-tire locks that fasten an outside tire to the body or frame of a recreational vehicle.
- ski locks that can be used to lock skis to each other, to a post outside a ski lodge, or to the top of a car.
- window locks that keep a thief from sliding open a window; also locks that prevent easy entry through a patio glass door.
- telephone-dial locks for older, rotary phones: a little plug that locks onto the phone and prevents the dial from turning, thus limiting long-distance calls or use of a phone without permission. (I haven't seen a lock system for a push-button phone, though it can always be locked in a desk drawer.)
- gun locks: oval metal locks that slip into the trigger guard of a gun and prevent it from being fired.
- trailer locks that fit into the hitch of a trailer, preventing a person from simply hooking up a trailer and driving off with it.
- steering-wheel locks, shaped like a cane, that can be wedged into the steering wheel to prevent it from turning; even if

thieves break into a car and hot-wire it to start the engine, they can't drive away.

Unusual and interesting locks and keys can be found almost any place. For example the local pharmacy or drugstore will have bottles of pills with childproof caps. The cap won't open unless it is pressed down in a special way. The instructions are written on the top of the cap, but the assumption is that children who might get into the medicine and hurt themselves can't read. In this case *reading* proves to be the key that unlocks the cap.

In your wanderings, don't forget to look for interesting key chains and key holders. In addition to the fake-rock key holder to hide in the yard (see chapter 3), you may also find magnetic key boxes to hide a spare key somewhere in a car, key chains that break into parts so you can leave a key with somebody else, key markers so you can tell at a glance which key to use, and even a key ring with a built-in electronic device that beeps when you clap your hands, allowing you to find keys you've misplaced around the house.

5 What's in a Word?

By definition a lock is simply a device for fastening or closing things, and a key is a tool for opening a lock.

But words often mean much more than their simple dictionary definitions, and one can tell a great deal about the importance of locks and keys by seeing how the words have been used in our language.

The English language is over fifteen hundred years old (with root, or ancestor, languages that go back much further than that). Words for *lock* and *key* turn up in the very oldest writings in English. *Locu* (pronounced low-koo) is an Old English word for "lock" from Old High German, an ancestor language. In one of the early texts we read of "Godes engel" (God's angel) who "undyde" (undid, or opened) a "locu" to let a person into heaven. Another early text tells of a man who was a "lokismith" or "lock smyth" who could "unpik hus lockes" (unpick his locks). Apparently, then as now, if you lost a key, you could get help from a locksmith.

The word *key* first appears in English as *caeg*, coming into the language from an old Germanic word, *keige*, or "spear." (A key *is* a bit like a spear, isn't it?) *Key* was often spelled ''keye,'' and in early English it was pronounced kay.

Language experts have several notions about the word *padlock.* One theory grows from the early English meaning of *pad* as ''basket.'' A padlockke, then, was something a person could carry around, portably, like a basket or in a basket. However, some people think that the connection of *padlock* with *basket* grew from the fact that a basket with a handle looks a lot like a padlock. Still others believe the connection might have come from the use of a padlockke to hold baskets and boxes onto the back of a wagon. Yet another interpretation argues that *pads* was also a slang expression for highway robbers, who hung around the public footpaths, or footpads. A padlockke, then, was a device to foil these robbers.

Words ''Unlocked''

> Under the willow tree
> two doves cry, ah, oh!
> Where shall we sleep, my love,
> whither shall we fly?
> The wood has swallowed the moon,
> the fog has swallowed the shore,
> the green toad has swallowed
>   the key to my door.
>   —Gian Carlo Menotti

Often in our language we ''unlock'' the strict meaning of a word and use it as a metaphor, or figure of speech. Gian Carlo Menotti's song about doves lost in a fog also tells about people and how they feel when they are lost. We can become lost in physical space—in the city, in the mountains, in the forest—but we can also be lost emotionally: confused, hurt, not knowing where to go or what to do next. When we feel lost and can't escape or find our way, it is as if an evil ''green toad'' has ''swallowed'' the key to our door. The fog, the toad, the wood all serve as metaphors to explain more than words alone can tell.

To give another example: Because the human heart is seen as a center of life, it has often been used as a metaphor for emotions like love and sadness and hate and friendship. "I gave my heart to my love." "I come to you with a heavy heart." On Valentine's Day, in particular, we give heart-shaped cards and heart-shaped candy to girlfriends and boyfriends to show them our affection. Of course we know that these are not real hearts. We prefer the metaphorical red heart to the blood-and-guts real thing.

We can see hearts, locks, and keys all used as metaphors in this little verse by the poet John O'Reilly:

> You gave me the key to your heart, my love:
>   Then why do you make me knock?

A young man is puzzled. His girlfriend "unlocked" her emotions and told him she loved him. But then something happened, and he found himself metaphorically locked out, pounding at the door; his key wouldn't work anymore. The girl replies:

> Oh, that was yesterday; Saints above,
>   Last night I changed the lock!

The poem is called "Constancy," and O'Reilly is using an example of lock and key to show how lovers' emotions can change overnight.

Another poet, Bertha Backus, would advise the young man not to take this rejection too seriously. Get yourself a lockbox, or chest, she suggests:

> Lock all your heartaches within it,
>   Then sit on the lid and laugh.

The word *lock*, then, can mean much more than a small machine to fasten your front door or your bicycle or your secret diary. A lock can be:

- a set of gates on a canal or river that raise or lower the water by locking in the water or letting it flow to another level. (The locks on the Panama Canal, for instance, allow ships to climb over mountains 280 feet high while traveling between the Atlantic and Pacific oceans.)

- a move in wrestling where you lock, or hold, opponents so they cannot move. (The poet John Milton once wrote of practicing "all the locks and gripes [grips] of wrestling.")
- a person who receives stolen goods. (This person is sometimes also called a fence.) Also, a lock is the name of the place where such a person stashes the stolen property out of sight.
- a railway signal that prevents one train from going on tracks occupied by another train.
- a financial agreement that guarantees, or locks in, a deal, letting two people agree on a price or a rate of interest.
- a compartment in a submarine or spaceship—an air lock— that is pressurized, locking out water or the vacuum of outer space, providing a way for people to enter or leave the vessel.

You can find the word *lock* coming up in all areas of human affairs, often used as a metaphor for closing things down or preventing things from escaping.

In the sport of rugby, for example, the lock-man links arms with two buddies, and the three run down the field, arm-in-arm, knocking down opponents. (The same sort of lock has been banned in American football, where it was called the flying wedge.) After a tough game of football or rugby, the players' joints may become stiff and lock up. When the athletes take off their gear, they put it in a locker, and you may have a locker at school where you can safely lock up books, clothing, and a year's supply of candy wrappers and old bubble gum. You've no doubt heard of Davy Jones's Locker, which is somewhere in the depths of the sea. We don't know exactly who Davy Jones was, but his locker is where you wind up if you are drowned.

In dueling with swords, one person can lock the opponent's sword arm, pinning it so the other person can't get the blade free for a stab. When antlered animals fight by butting heads, sometimes they lock horns and cannot separate; that expression has come to represent any fight, including verbal arguments between people. If neither person can see the other's point of view, each can be said to be locked in to a particular position or way of thinking.

Before the age of computers, a typesetter would lock up a tray of lead type, wedging in bits of wood so the type would not fall out when the tray was moved or carried. In the newspaper business, when the evening or morning edition is all set, ready to be printed, that issue is said to be locked up, meaning that no more changes can be made.

In the military, soldiers march together in a lockstep, and this expression has evolved to symbolize people who all think the same way, who are engaged in lock-step thinking. In earlier times, when soldiers used guns that had to be loaded by hand, the mechanism that set off the powder was called a firelock or flintlock or matchlock, and that led to our expression lock, stock, and barrel, meaning "the whole thing." Also in the military, a person using a radar screen to hunt down an enemy vehicle or vessel will lock in a target (an expression we also use with television viewing, where we lock in a good picture for clarity and color).

When cars jam the streets and nobody can move, we have a case of gridlock. In medicine the disease of tetanus causes the jaw muscles to tighten up and is called lockjaw. We also think of a locked jaw as a symbol for keeping quiet, and one of the old texts advises a person to keep his or her mouth "shutte with the dore of sylence, & locked with the key of discrecyoun" (*discretion* means "common sense," so the advice is unlock one's mouth to speak carefully and thoughtfully). The English writer Thomas Carlyle said, "I keep a lock upon my lips," meaning that he could keep a secret safely. In elementary school, teachers often have kids pretend to lock their lips when there's too much noise in the class.

Locking and unlocking doors can be a symbol of hospitality (or the lack of it). In colonial days, when locks were expensive to come by or made by hand at the blacksmith's forge, many people simply latched their doors from the inside, running a string through a hole to the outside. To welcome a person, you would "leave the latchstring out," so he or she could enter your home. At night and in the presence of strangers, the string would be drawn inside, blocking entrance.

"Open locks, whoever knocks," says Macbeth in Shakespeare's play, anticipating the arrival of some people who can help him with his goals and ambitions. On the other hand you've heard of "locking the barn door after the cow's gotten out," taking action too late to prevent a loss or a theft.

Any time you want to restrain something or keep it from coming undone, you may think of locks. A knot at the end of a row of knitting is called a lockstitch, since it keeps the threads from unraveling. A locket is a small compartment where you hide or preserve a photograph of your loved one, or possibly even keep a lock of his or her hair. A locknut is a device to keep a nut from working loose, while an oarlock, or rowlock, is a bracket that keeps the oar of a rowboat from slipping. (A common trick at camp is to send a new kid looking for "the keys to the oarlocks," for of course there aren't any.)

Getting back to our theme of hearts, love, and locks, we know that for better or worse, when two people get married, they are said to enter wedlock. When lovers cling to each other tightly, they are said to be locked in an embrace. In medieval times, if parents didn't want their daughter to see a young man, they might literally lock her in a tower. But Christopher Marlowe wrote in 1590 that this strategy seldom worked, for when a young woman was "lock'd up in a brazen tower," the young man "desir'd her all the more." And there is an old saying: "Love laughs at locksmiths," meaning that young people in love have all sorts of ways of getting to see each other, even when their parents have forbidden it.

The Key As Metaphor

Like the word *lock, key* also has a range of metaphorical and symbolic meanings.

Keys are important because they have the power to unlock doors and gates and let people in to restricted places. The person who holds a key also holds a symbol of power. At a time when the human race was behaving badly, the poet Lord Byron wrote:

Saint Peter sat by the celestial gate:
His keys were rusty, and the lock was dull.

In our prison systems the jailer, or jail attendant, is slangingly called a turnkey, for he or she also has great power to set people free or to keep them in the lockup. You've probably seen numerous western movies where the hero, jailed for the wrong reason, manages to get the keys from the turnkey to make an escape. In real life, if prisoners rebel or riot, their freedom to move around inside the jail is stopped; they are kept in their cells in what is called a lockdown.

In the African country of Zaire a police officer doesn't wear a badge but carries keys as a symbol of power. In England *the king's keys* is slang for a crowbar, because the king's officers didn't need keys—they could break down any door they wanted.

In our time we have key clubs, where proof of membership is a key that lets members unlock the door. Frequently hotels will print guest passes to the restaurant or the pool, and even though there are no locks involved, the pass may be printed in the shape of a key or carry a picture of a key.

When an important person comes to town, we may give him or her a symbolic key, the key to the city. This dates back to the Middle Ages when cities were surrounded by walls and locked gates. If you gave somebody the key to the city, you were letting that person inside, showing a high measure of trust. When Governor William Penn arrived in New York in 1682, he was given a set of keys to the military fortifications, showing that he was a person honored and trusted. By contrast, *to put the key under the door* means to lock everyone out by placing the key on the inside—a lockup of a key in the manner of the locked-room mysteries discussed in chapter 4.

It is *not* complimentary to say that you are giving somebody the keys to the street; it means you are kicking the person out into the street where of course you don't need any keys at all. Once wandering the streets, keyless, you might run across a person who has a keyhold, or gotten drunk, which might be why that person has the keys to the street in the first place.

We often speak of the keys to success, that is, the secrets that will let us unlock the puzzle of how to get ahead in life. One way people have tried to achieve success is through the use of a silver key or gold key, meaning a bribe, a gift of gold or silver to make somebody give special or even illegal privileges.

In music a key is a set of notes linked together to create tuneful melodies. If you know that a piece is written in the key of C or G-sharp or B-flat, you have the secret to knowing how the scale is played. The English composer John Dowland explained in 1609, "A key is the opening of a Song, because like a Key opens a dore, so doth it the Song." The musical key is shown by a key signature, or *clef* (the French word for "key"), which unlocks information about how to read the music. In public speaking we often talk of the keynote address, a speech that, like the first movement of a musical work, sounds the opening theme.

Music also uses the word *key* for various kinds of buttons and valves on instruments; these keys obviously unlock the music hidden away in the instrument. A clarinet or flute or oboe has dozens of keys that open air holes, changing the notes, creating lovely music or ordinary scales depending on the skill of the key opener. The keys of a piano strike levers that bang on piano wires; the keys of an accordion open small metal valves; the keys of older pipe organs are linked to flappers that let air into the pipes; the keys of newer organs and synthesizers are wired to electronic sound-generating devices. One keyboard instrument, the clavichord, even gets its name from the Latin word *clavis*, which means "little key."

In chess the key is an opening move that starts a match. If you can guess at or read your opponent's key, you can unlock his or her strategy and figure out what to do next.

In football a quarterback will key on a defense, or read the keys, looking for signs that will let him figure out how to call a play that will thwart the defense. Football announcers often speak of a key set of downs, which means a series of plays that will unlock victory or lock a team into defeat, and players are likely to be keyed up for those key plays. The expression *keyed up* comes from the use of keys as a way to wind up old-fashioned, spring-driven clocks; so it means "wound up tight as a spring," ready to explode into action. In turn keyed up has been adapted to music, where it describes the process of singing or playing music higher than usual to give it a more intense sound.

A telegraph key opens a flow of electricity and lets the telegrapher send messages through a wire. A typewriter or computer keyboard serves the same sort of function, unlocking the electricity so it creates a letter or number on the page. From these uses we get words like *keyboarding skills* (for learning how to use a computer) and *keypad* (a cluster of keys for punching in numbers). As we'll see in chapter 6, computers are often used to control locking mechanisms in doors, so that gradually the keys on a computer are coming to replace the metal key that you insert in a lock.

In construction a keystone is a stone or brick that is placed at the center of an arch; if the keystone is removed, the whole structure will collapse. So we often speak of keystone ideas or people, without which the best laid plan may fall apart. This meaning has expanded to baseball, where the keystone corner, third base, is seen as a special place, a key to the success of the defense.

Open Sesame!

Words themselves can serve as keys to unlock entrances. In the *Tales of the Arabian Nights,* the phrase *Open Sesame* is used to gain entrance to the treasure room. It is a word, like *Abracadabra,* that unlocks the world of magic. A similar kind of unlocking word is a *shibboleth.* In the Bible the Book of Judges tells of the people of the tribe of Ephraim, who were identified as strangers because they had difficulty pronouncing that word—the "th" sound was not in their language. In our time, a shibboleth is a test of sorts. An excellent example of this is what people call the city of San Francisco. Don't ever call that place 'Frisco, at least not in the presence of a San Franciscan, for right away, you show that you are not a member of that community. In fact people who are *really* in the know simply call it "The City," for Californians know that you mean the place strangers call 'Frisco, not New York (the "Big Apple" to those in the know) or Chicago (*not* "Chi-town" but always "Chicago"—or possibly "Chicagoland").

The reverse of a shibboleth is a taboo word, one that we ordinarily *don't* use in polite conversation. If you utter a taboo word, you quickly find yourself locked out of a conversation.

Sometimes people even use words to deliberately exclude others. Jargon is complex language that is used by members of a group, sometimes to keep other people locked out. If somebody says, "I had to dump my floppies and reinitialize the hard drive after the virus wiped out my data," you might or might not recognize that he or she is speaking computerese, a form of jargon. As long ago as 1550, a man complained, "The worst man of all is that will mak himself a locke of words and speach, which is known not to be in my faction." The complainer was feeling excluded because people would not use words that let him in on the conversation.

Sometimes a group will use its own slang (or argot, pronounced R-go) to keep other people locked on the outside. You may have done it yourself: At one time or another an adult has probably said to you, "Don't use all that slang with me. I don't know what you're talking about."

Of course you know about passwords and have probably used or invented some yourself—a word or phrase that you memorize—showing that you are a member of a group and want to have doors unlocked.

"Halt! Who goes there?" demands the military sentry. The person approaching may have to identify him or herself with a password or "word of the day."

A particularly famous and ancient password—or pass-conversation, you might say—happens daily in England. At the Tower of London, a Ceremony of the Keys has been taking place for over seven hundred years. At exactly 9:53 P.M. the Chief Warder makes the final rounds of the tower area. (Remember that a *warded* lock is one protected against false entry, so a warder is sort of a guard, or protector.) As part of his job, he locks all the gates. When he arrives at the Bloody Tower, where so many English rulers lost their heads, he is confronted by a sentry.

"Who goes there?"

"The keys," answers the Warder, identifying himself by the keys he carries.

"Whose keys?" demands the sentry.

"Queen Elizabeth's keys," replies the Warder, giving the password.

"Advance Queen Elizabeth's keys," the sentry says. "All's well."

In the world of computers, passwords are commonly used to lock out someone who is not supposed to be using the system. The computer asks for a password, and once that secret word is given, the programs and files can be opened. A computer password can be a word, a phrase, or a series of numbers. Some computer hackers have realized that people will often choose a familiar or easily remembered name or number for a password: the name of a boyfriend or wife, the date of a child's birth, one's Social Security number. It's possible, then, to guess a password. Some computer hackers have even developed programs that systematically test out passwords or code sequences on systems they want to penetrate. A computer can try millions of passwords, perhaps hitting on the right one by mere luck, a process that would take a human being a lifetime of guessing.

Passwords are thus as valuable as keys themselves. It's possible for people up to no good to intercept or learn a password. The crude way to do this (as you've seen on television) is to capture a person and threaten harm or violence unless he or she gives up the word. With more subtlety, one can eavesdrop on a conversation, stand near the entryway to overhear the password, or look over a person's shoulder while he or she is typing in a password. Thus word keys can be lost or misused almost as easily as metal keys.

Locking Up Words

Words themselves are often precious and secret in other ways as well. When the United States government built a new embassy in Moscow, it discovered that Russian contractors had managed to install electronic bugs in the walls so spies could listen in on secret conversations. There are several ways to defeat bugs, including creating a masking noise, making electrical interference, or finding ways to disable the electronic system. In the case of the United States embassy, however, the bugs were so many and planted so deeply in the walls that the United States government gave up and built a new building. In effect, it discovered there was no way to lock up its words safely.

Secret codes are one of the oldest and most popular methods for locking up words. Codes can be very simple or complex. Here is a simple code (interestingly enough, the solution is called a key) that allows you to substitute one letter for another so that you come up with a message that looks like gibberish. You type or write the alphabet twice with different letters facing one another.

A B C D E F G H I J K L M N O P Q R S T U V W X Y Z
B C D E F G H I J K L M N O P Q R S T U V W X Y Z A

The word *gibberish* becomes:

H-J-C-C-F-S-J-T-I

A professional wouldn't have much difficulty breaking this code, partly because there is only a one-letter difference between the real message and its gibber-code. Still, try this with a friend and you'll probably see that the key is not easily discovered.

However, simple codes or ciphers that substitute one letter for another are easily cracked, the code world's equivalent of lockpicking. We know, for example, that the most common letter in the English language is *e*, so it may be that the most frequently appearing letter in a substitution code stands for *e*. We also recognize that in English, vowels show up in certain places in words, and we know what kinds of letters show up at the ends of words. As one plays with lockpicking a code, one starts to get bits and pieces of a message and can possibly figure out the rest simply by guessing.

A famous code developed by Frenchman Blaise de Vignere uses substitutions—one letter for another—but makes exchanges based on a secret phrase or password chosen in advance by two communicators. The Vignerian Cipher is one that is extremely difficult to decode because you have to know a password and the code itself in order to make it work.

Words and information can also be hidden within puzzles and riddles or as clues. Edgar Allan Poe's famous story, "The Gold Bug," is basically about figuring out where a treasure is hidden based on a set of clues. You've probably been on a treasure hunt yourself where, by decoding clues, you can find rewards. You may have played word games or puzzles in the newspaper where you unscramble words, and once they're unscrambled, you can unscramble a sentence that gives you interesting or secret information.

Electronics have also gotten into the act of locking up speech. Instead of secret codes, the military and even some business operations now use voice scrambles to give secrecy to telephone conversations. As you speak, a computer breaks your message into bits and pieces and rearranges their order before sending them through the wire. Scramblers can also change the pitch of a message and even send several messages at the same time, all mixed together. A decoding device at the other end then puts the message back together so that one can hold a normal conversation without even being aware of the way the voices have been chopped up and reassembled along the way. Of course, you'd better be certain your office isn't bugged, or the message can be stolen anyway.

As we'll see in the next chapter, electronic equipment adds a whole new dimension to locks and locksmithing. Even the words *lock* and *key* are changing. Sometimes nowadays you'll hear of "access-control systems" instead of locks and keys. Somehow that new phrase will never substitute for the elegance, simplicity, and historical traditions of *locke* and *keye*.

6 Locks for an Electronic Age

Always lock up a Cat in a Closet where you keep your China Plates, for fear the mice may steal in and break them.

This bit of advice, given in 1745 by Jonathan Swift (author of *Gulliver's Travels*) is witty, but not very practical. A cat may protect your fine plates from an invasion of mice, but it is likely to head for the hills if a real burglar threatens.

Although animal and human guards have proven successful for some aspects of security, for most of the last five thousand years human beings have depended on small machines—locks—to fend off burglars. Until recently, these locks and keys have been *mechanical*. That is they rely on muscle and cogs and gears and bolts and latches to get the job done. You turn a key that turns a gear that throws a bolt that blocks or unblocks your door. Whether we're talking about the original Egyptian wooden locks, a modern Kryptonite bike lock, or the combination lock on your school locker, mechanical principles make the lock work.

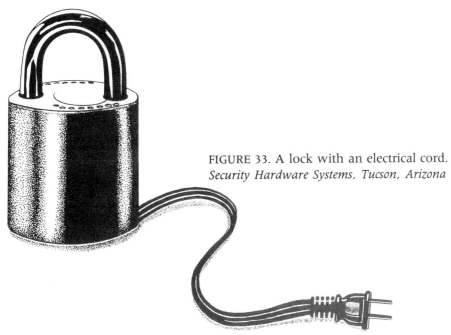

FIGURE 33. A lock with an electrical cord.
Security Hardware Systems, Tucson, Arizona

However, as electricity has been tamed in the past several hundred years, leading to successful electric motors, lights, toasters, doorbells, and battery-powered bunnies—to name just a few of its accomplishments—locksmiths have looked to electrical power as a way of locking things up, in, and out.

In the 1870s, for example, James Sargent found a way to link the mechanical locks on his safes to electrically powered clocks, leading to the time-delay vault that is in every bank in the country today. (See Figure 33.) As early as 1886, one D. Rousseau filed a patent application for an Electrical Door Opener that was designed for apartment buildings.

Electric and Magnetic Locks

There are many ways in which electricity can be used to power both locks and keys. One of the most visible is a system that you've probably seen often and been tempted to test out; it's one of those exit bars that say:

IN EMERGENCY PUSH TO OPEN.
ALARM WILL SOUND.

Resist temptation. Don't push on the bars *except* in an emergency, for, yes, the alarm *will* sound.

When emergency exit systems were first designed they were mostly mechanical. When the so-called panic bar was pushed, a mechanical door latch was released and set off an alarm (powered by electricity). The newer systems are all electric, and the lock itself is *electromagnetic*.

You've no doubt experimented with magnets, and you know that two magnets exert an attraction for each other. You may also have worked with electromagnets, where an electric current magnetizes a piece of steel, and when the current is disconnected, the steel is demagnetized. In an electromagnetic lock, a magnet in the door is attracted to a piece of steel in the door frame; as long as current is flowing, the door will remain locked.

It might seem improbable to you that an electromagnet could hold a door shut. Couldn't you just lean on the door and overpower the magnet? But think of the strength of electromagnets you've seen on TV: the kind that can lift an automobile weighing several tons. It's relatively easy to create a small electromagnet that requires a thousand to three thousand pounds of shoulder pressure to open the door. You'd be better off renting an elephant than trying to open the door yourself. The electromagnetic emergency lock effectively keeps the door locked from the outside but allows anybody inside to escape, for now when the panic bar is hit, the supply of electricity to the electromagnet is cut and, presto, the door can be pushed open by a lamb rather than an elephant. The alarm, of course, simply lets security people know that the door has been opened. That way they can be certain that nobody sneaks *in* the now-opened door. Maybe they're smuggling in elephants, or, more likely, trying to smuggle out goods during the commotion over the alarm.

Different kinds of electrical locks are now used in all sorts of installations, mostly in large office buildings, apartments, hospitals, and schools, but increasingly in homes as well. Sometimes electricity is used to turn a small motor or a gizmo called a solenoid that withdraws the bolt in a door; sometimes the electricity goes to the strike that engages the bolt, with electromagnets to withdraw the strike and let people enter.

With electrical locks there is always a worry about power failure. What happens if the power goes off? Electric lock systems are of two different types: fail secure and fail safe. A fail *secure* system keeps the door *locked* in the event of a loss of power—that is, you can't unlock the door while the power is off. Such systems are mainly used to protect valuables during the blackout, keeping them secure. A fail *safe* system protects people by leaving the door *unlocked* during the power failure, thus not trapping people inside their house or apartment or school.

Electronic Keys and Access Control

Any lock system needs a tool to operate it: a key. And here is where the use of electricity becomes especially interesting, for it opens the way to electronic systems. In contrast to an *electric* lock, which uses power to bolt and unbolt the door, an *electronic* system is based on computers and sends signals to the lock to open it, provided the right key is used. And electronic systems, in turn, are revolutionizing the meaning of the word *key*.

One of the age old complaints about mechanical locks and keys is that the keys are easily lost or stolen, making security difficult. For example lost keys have long been a headache for hotels. Frequently guests will forget to turn in the key to a room when they check out. What is the hotel to do? Of course it can create a new key for the lock, and often hotels have a key-making machine somewhere in the basement for this purpose. Soon, though, they have lots of extra keys floating around. It would be easy for a thief to check into a room for a day, walk off with the key, wait until that room is occupied by somebody else, and then use the "lost" key to gain access. As a hotelkeeper, one could make it a policy to change the lock every time a key disappears, but that process is time-consuming and expensive.

Electronic systems now provide an alternative. One of these, Saflok, is shown in Figure 34. The Saflok key is a plastic card with a magnetic stripe on the back, the same kind that appears on credit and bank cards. When a person checks into a hotel, a computer-driven device at the front desk creates a code on the magnetic stripe. Upstairs, the door lock to the hotel room includes a magnetic strip reader and an electromagnetic lock. If the code on the card matches the code in the lock, the door is electromagnetically unlocked for about six seconds, and a green light flashes, signaling the card user to enter. Every guest gets a new card and a new code. In fact the system is designed so that whenever a new card with the proper code is inserted in the lock, the code for the previous user is wiped out of the access system. With this system the hotel can easily change the lock—or, more accurately, change the lock code—every time a new customer checks in. If somebody walks off with a Saflok key, it's no loss to the hotel. Saflok also includes a system for master keying, so maids, security officers, and other hotel officials can have access to rooms.

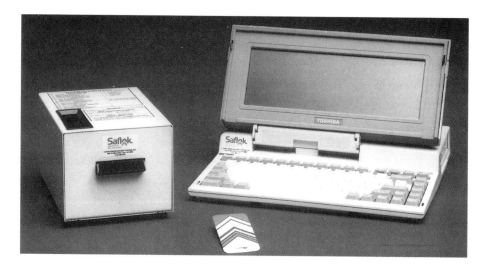

FIGURE 34. An electronic key system with computer, plastic key-card, and a card encoding device. *Saflok Control Security Systems, Inc., Troy, Michigan*

Saflok is not the only company in the electronic key business. This industry is very competitive, with a number of different companies in the market offering systems. For example some manufacturers have built systems around push buttons in the door mechanism. You punch in your number code, and if it is an authorized number, either recognized by a minicomputer in the lock itself or by a master computer somewhere in the building, the door will open. An advantage to this system is that there is no key or card to lose. A trouble spot is that people can forget their codes, or a person peering over someone's shoulder can learn the code and gain false entry. To solve the latter problem, some push-button systems have a security shield, a small shade that covers the buttons and hides them from prying eyes.

Bank money machines use both a magnetic card and a punch-in code to unlock the system and allow one to take out funds. When you put your card into the machine, it "reads" the magnetic stripe and asks you to punch in your personal identification number, or PIN. Unless your PIN matches the computer's records, you will be denied access to the machine.

Another kind of electronic key system uses bar codes—the narrow stripes you see on food packages. Your key is encoded with a bar code; an infrared bar code reader is installed near the door, and you run your key card past the reader to gain access. However, a bar code key is easily copied, even by a photocopy machine, so illegal keys can be produced.

Some electronic keys have the code embedded in the plastic rather than as a magnetic stripe or bar code. These keys are held up to an electronic sensor to trigger the door. The Handykey system, for example, uses an electronic touch pad, shown on the left in Figure 35. Instead of being inserted into a lock or card reader, the plastic key is merely held up to the image of an old-fashioned mechanical key. A computer system keeps track of keys and codes, so many people can have access to the system. If somebody moves or quits his or her job, the number of that person's key is simply zapped from the computer memory. That way security people in apartments, businesses, and schools don't have to rekey locks every time a person leaves the system.

FIGURE 35. A Handykey (the small dark plastic "tag") and its electronic sensor pad. *Handykey, Salinas, California*

Multiple Security Systems

Words like *lock* and *key* start to have an old-fashioned sound to them when one looks at electronic security systems. The new systems do a lot more than simply let people in and out. For example an electronic system that identifies a magnetic card or plastic key can also be programmed to keep track of when a person entered a building. Every time a card is used, an entry is made in the computer log, so some businesses are now using their entry system as a way of keeping track of who comes and goes. (You may recall from chapter 2 that, long ago, mechanical counter locks could tell a person if his or her lock had been opened. The newer systems not only tell that the lock has been opened, but who did it.) In fact the computers can even be linked to the pass card an employee uses to get into the parking lot, so the boss could have a record of the employee's comings and goings from the moment he or she drove into the lot. It's a bit scary, actually, to realize how much information is stored in electronic systems of this kind, and some people are concerned that electronics can lead to an invasion of privacy: that it's possible for people to know too much about you from the electronic trail you leave with your plastic access cards.

The situation is even more complicated when one realizes that several different kinds of electronic systems can be linked together, not only for entry, but for surveillance. Many businesses and industries are now using television cameras, motion detectors, and various kinds of alarm systems in combination with electronic locks and keys. Such systems not only limit access to people who have the right electronic keys, but patrol the hallways, corridors, and even the parking lot looking for people who shouldn't be there in the first place. (See Figure 36.)

Many of these access-control systems are quite expensive and can only be used by businesses with large numbers of employees. However, systems are being developed for home use. For example many companies now sell security packages that include a push-button or card-access lock system, heat and smoke detectors, motion sensors, and a "help" button, connected by phone lines to a headquarters where, twenty-four hours a day, people watch for trouble. If an intruder tries to get past a system or manages to get into the house or apartment or if a fire breaks out or if someone is sick or thinks there's a burglar in the house, the switchboard at the central station lights up and somebody sends help.

The World of Biometrics

But there's more!

As sophisticated as some of these electronic key systems are, they still have *keys*, and keys can become lost or stolen. Of course a combination lock or a punch-in system doesn't use a key, but a person can still forget the combination or PIN. Lockmakers have long been dreaming about systems that would work without keys, where doors open by magic— "Open Sesame"—as the right person walks along.

You've seen this kind of keyless world in many science fiction television shows and movies.

"Computer!" says the captain of the starship. "Open the doors to the secret planning room."

FIGURE 36. The outer fringe of an access-control system: a fence wired to detect someone breaking in or climbing over. *Litton Poly-Scientific, Inc., Blacksburg, Virginia*

"Yes, Captain Star," replies the computer. *It has recognized the captain's voice* and will let him, and him alone, into the top secret room.

Or we see the starship's senior officer walk up to a sensor, place a palm on the panel, and the door opens. *The sensor has recognized the officer's palm print* and used that as a key to the door.

What's surprising is that many of the systems you see in science fiction are actually under development, and many of them are operating in the world today. They're called *biometric* (from *bio*, meaning "living" and *metric*, meaning "to measure"). Biometrics, then, is based on measurements, or "keys" taken from human beings.

To illustrate how a biometric system works, let's take one of your unique features, your nose. There isn't another one exactly like it in the universe. How could we use your nose as a key in a biometric system?

To begin with, we might take photographs or video scans of your nose from a profile view. We would then take measurements. In the simplified sketch of Figure 37, the nose is measured from the top to bottom (its height) and at four places from side to side (how far it sticks out from your face).

Now, in the future, when you come to the door, a scanner looks at your nose profile, and the measurements are compared to those on file. Because your nose is one of a kind, the computer will recognize your measurements and open the door.

Suppose somebody else comes to the door, say, your worst enemy. He or she will have a nose profile scanned, but because this second nose doesn't fit a pattern the computer has on file, the door will not open.

But suppose one day you've been in a fight or walked face first into a door. Your nose is flattened or puffy. *Its measurements have changed.* The computer not only doesn't recognize you, it calls the police. This is called *false reject* and is one of the problems developers of biometric systems must deal with. And let's suppose, further, that your archenemy is your identical twin brother or sister. His or her nose may be so close to yours in measurements that the computer would welcome him or her home. This is a *false accept,* and it, too, is a problem for biometrics.

Actually, the nose *isn't* such a great object to measure, partly because

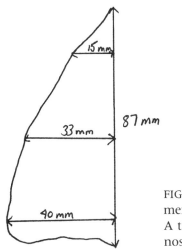

FIGURE 37. Measuring the nose. The five measurements shown give the computer a profile to study. A true biometric system might measure the same nose in dozens of places to get a more detailed profile.

a nose *can* get broken or puffed or swollen. Furthermore, many people would object to having to stick their noses into some sort of scanning instrument every morning coming into work or every evening to get in their front door. (You can imagine that the scanning device would soon pick up nicknames like The Sniffer Sniffer or The Schnozz Gobbler.) There are other body features that can be used more conveniently and with higher reliability to serve as a key. In practice, too, biometric systems take many more than just five measurements. With a biometric scanner it's possible to take dozens, even hundreds of measurements almost instantly, giving the computer a huge volume of information to work with.

What follow are some examples of biometric systems that are in practical use today.

Signature Catchers

For a long time human beings have recognized that each person's signature is unique. Thus we use signatures on checks, contracts, and all sorts of legal documents. In fact even before computers, banks used signatures as a sort of biometric system: People would put a copy of their John Hancock on file, and a bank teller would compare a new signature to the original to see if they were the same. It has been a pretty good system, but not foolproof. One can, of course, forge signatures with enough accuracy so that a teller cannot distinguish between the real one and the copy.

In biometrics the signature system becomes both more complicated and more reliable. The Sign/On system (see Figure 38) uses an electronic signature tablet coupled with a computer. A person signs his or her name in the usual way on a piece of paper placed on the tablet. However, the tablet doesn't actually record the *shape* of the signature. Rather, using two scanners, it makes a record of the *motions* and *movements* of the pen as the person writes. It records how fast the person writes, how high he or she lifts the pen off the page, even how the person dots an *i* or crosses a *t*. These movements are recorded in the computer, measured, and turned into numbers. In the future, when the person comes in, the computer compares the motions in memory to the new motions and decides

FIGURE 38. A Sign/On tablet recording signature movements. *Digital Signatures, Inc., Columbia, Maryland*

whether this is the right person or not. A forger, then, might be able to duplicate a signature exactly, but it is very unlikely he or she could copy the hand movement. Furthermore, every time a person signs on to the system, it takes and records new measurements, adding these in with the old ones. So this computer learns more about the user every time it is given information. Thus if a signature changes over time—say as someone grows older—the computer automatically updates its memory and continues to give access.

Hands and Fingers

We've also known for a long time that human fingerprints are unique. Law enforcement agencies, from local police to Interpol, keep collections of fingerprints on file, and sophisticated systems of analysis make it possible to see if a set of prints comes from a particular person. So it is quite natural that a fingerprint key system would be developed.

To log on to a fingerprint system, the user sticks his or her finger into a hole or slot, and a scanner takes several readings of the fingerprint pattern. The measurements are added up or combined to create a set of data, or template, for the future. To use the system, the person plugs a finger into the scanner hole, and an image is taken and compared to the originals. If there is a match, the door opens for the person. Some problems with false rejections have been encountered with this system. If the weather is cold or hot or humid or dry, fingertips can pucker or expand by tiny amounts, throwing off the data.

Another system is based on a reading of a person's hand geometry. The HandKey (not to be confused with the Handykey, described earlier in this chapter) asks the user to place a hand on a platform, spreading out the fingers to fit a series of pegs. (See Figure 39.) The pegs simply guarantee that every time the system is used, the person puts his or her hand in the same place. A number of measurements are taken: the shape of the fingers, the position of the joints, the distances between various points of the hand. Like our imaginary nose scanner, this one uses a computer to compare stored data to the current measurement. If there's a match, the door opens. Although this machine seems rather like the sort of palm print reader you see in science fiction movies, it isn't looking at the pattern of ridges and whorls on the hand. (Maybe someday someone will invent a biometric machine that will not only record your palm print, but will tell your future by reading your palm as well.)

The Eyes Have It

The pattern of blood vessels in the back of your eye is as unique as your fingerprint! The retina, or film, of the eye can thus be used with extraordinary accuracy as a means of identifying a person. Like the other biometric systems, this one begins by having a new user log on. The person peers into an eyepiece, rather like some of the eye-testing machines used by optometrists. You line up your eye by looking at a lighted target; then the machine scans the eye, sending a beam of light to the retina and making a record of the reflections. In one retinal system, 320 different measurements are made (remember that in our nose scanner we took only 5). After this information is digested by the computer, the person's eye functions as a key. The system is practically error free. The pattern

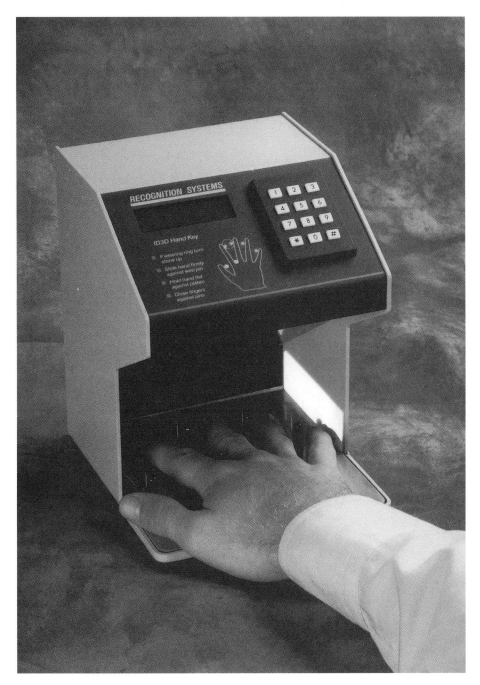

FIGURE 39. A HandKey system. *Recognition Systems, Inc., San Jose, California*

is so unique that the scanner and computer are almost never wrong. One problem reported with this system is that some users are nervous about having a beam of light sent into their eye every time they want to get into the system. But actually the system beams in no more light than what naturally enters their eyes on an ordinary day.

Hello. Is That You?

Your voice can even serve as a biometric key. A voice identification system listens to a person saying a phrase and creates a voice print or pattern. Actually, the system isn't listening to the words at all: It is recording a pattern of vibrations and taking measurements of their characteristics, almost as if it were measuring the shape of a nose. Although you might think a person could imitate your voice to beat the system, the voiceprint is biometrically unique. That is, even though two voices might sound the same to the human ear, the voiceprint reader would detect important differences and reject the imitation. The system will also *not* respond to a recorded voice, preventing entry by someone stealing your voice on tape. Like many other biometric systems, the voiceprint identifier is a *learning* system. It adds new measurements to its old data file and thus knows more and more about you every time you talk to it. If your voice changes with age, the computer will alter its pattern. In fact even if you have a cold or a sore throat or have been shouting during a sporting event, a voice identifier can recognize your voice with a high degree of accuracy.

The Future of Locksmithing

As you can see from this chapter, the nature of lock-and-key systems is changing very rapidly. Some of the other amazing systems now for sale include:

- a video entry system that allows you to see the face of a person before opening the door. (Remember that your one-and-only face is your most complex and interesting biometric feature.)

- an electronic push-button lock system with 29 million possible combinations.
- a structural vibration sensor that can sense whether a safe or vault is threatened by a burglar with a high-power drill.
- a glass-break detector that keeps burglars from avoiding the locks by simply breaking the glass.
- a home push-button access system that also turns up the heat in the house and provides an intercom device.
- a patrol robot that rolls up and down the hallways of a building looking for movement and sending radio and video reports back to a central station.

So locks and keys and access control are changing, and so is the business of locksmithing. Until recently the locksmith was mainly a specialist in mechanical systems. You would go to the locksmith for extra keys or to have a set of locks changed or to get a really secure system set up in your home. Nowadays a locksmith may be involved in selling and servicing a complex electronic system that includes locks, burglar alarms, and fire sensing equipment. Instead of working with padlocks and combination locks and pin tumbler locks, the locksmith may be more interested in wiring systems and computer chips.

If you talk to some people about the future of locks and keys, they tell of a biometric or electronic world where your voice or your palm print gets you in everyplace you should have access, or where you carry a single card that lets you into your home, your office, and the bank money machine.

Other people argue that the new electronic systems are quite expensive and claim that the good old mechanical lock and key are here to stay. It's a lot cheaper to buy a mechanical padlock, for example, than it is to buy an elaborate computer and a set of electronic sensors.

Gale Johnson, editor of *Locksmith Ledger* magazine, has written:

There is still a need for the traditional locksmith. Even the most complex electronic lock systems commonly use mechanical locks and keys as a backup. The relatively inexpensive cost and maintenance

of tumbler-style locks make them ideal for most low and medium
security applications.

Johnson wants the locksmith of the future to be called a *security technician*,
adding that the locksmith needs to change with the times and learn how
to use the electronic and biometric systems along with mechanical locks
and keys.

Time will tell, of course. Having read this history of locks and keys,
you are now in a good position to understand what's happening with
the traditional ways and the modern electronic ways of locking things
up, in, and out.

References

Alth, Max. *All About Locks and Locksmithing*. New York: Hawthorne, 1972.

Basala, George. *The Evolution of Technology*. Cambridge, Eng.: Cambridge University Press, 1988.

"Bicycle Locks." *Consumer Reports*. December 1981, 374–378.

Briggs, Noel Currier. *Contemporary Observations from the Chubb Collection, 1818–1968*. London: Chubb & Sons Lock and Safe Co., Ltd., 1968.

Buehr, Walter. *The Story of Locks*. New York: Charles Scribner's Sons, 1953.

Caggiano, Chris. "Keyless Office Security." *INC*. November 1991, 202.

"Charters of Freedom." Washington, D.C.: National Archives Records Administration, n.d.

Crichton, Whitcomb. *Practical Course in Modern Locksmithing*. Chicago: Nelson-Hall, 1969.

Daumas, Maurice, ed. *A History of Technology and Invention*. New York: Crown, 1969.

Eco, Umberto, and G. B. Zorzoli. *The Picture History of Inventions*. New York: Macmillan, 1963.

Eras, Vincent. *Locks and Keys Throughout the Ages*. Dordrecht, Netherlands: Lips' Safe and Lock Manufacturing Company, 1957.

Fennelly, Lawrence J., ed. *Handbook of Loss Prevention and Crime Prevention*. Boston: Butterworth, 1982.

Gardner, J. Starkie. *Iron Work*. London: Victoria and Albert Museum, 1927.

Gunkel, Klaus. "Tute Sekreta Kiel Cifri Tekstojn." *Monato.* September 1989, 28–29.

Hogg, Gary. *Safe Bind, Safe Find.* New York: Criterion, 1968.

Holmes, James P., Larry Wright, and Russell Maxwell. "Scandia Tests Error Rates of Biometric Tools." *Access Control.* February 1992, 1, 14–18.

Illustrated Catalogue and Price List, Vol. 31. Terryville, Conn.: Eagle Lock Company, 1914.

Johnson, Gale. "Signs of Change." *Locksmith Ledger/Security Technician.* June 1991, 4, 43.

Jones, Maurice. "The Fascination of the Lock." Hamilton, Ohio: Mosler, Inc. 1988.

Key Locks and Door Bolts: Illustrated Catalog. Rochester, N.Y.: Sargent, Greenleaf & Brooks, 1895.

Lambert, Lori. "Just What Is Access Control?" *Keynotes.* February 1992, 22–23.

Landels, J. G. *Engineering in the Ancient World.* Berkeley, Cal.: University of California Press, 1978.

Lock and Hardware (Catalog 22). New York: Yale & Towne Manufacturing Company, 1917.

"Michael Zane's Kryptonite Lock." *People Weekly.* April 30, 1984, 79.

Monk, Eric. *Keys: Their History and Collection.* Aylesbury, Bucks, Eng.: Shire Publications, 1979.

Nieves, Evelyn. "When Crime Can't Be Worse, Then Sales Can't Be Better." *New York Times.* October 8, 1990, A14, B3.

Olmert, Michael. "Points of Origin." *Smithsonian,* February 1985, 42–44.

O'Toole, George. *The Private Sector: Private Spies, Rent-a-Cops, and the Police-Industrial Complex.* New York: W. W. Norton, 1978.

Phillips, Bill. *Professional Locksmithing Techniques.* Blue Ridge Summit, Penn.: TAB Books, 1991.

Robbins, Michael W. "All about Locks and Alarms." *New York.* February 8, 1982, 27–31.

Rosberg, Robert. "History of Mosler." *Mpulse.* March 1973.

Sloane, Eugene. *The Complete Book of Locks, Keys, Burglar and Smoke Alarms and Other Security Devices.* New York: William Morrow, 1977.

"Where to Hide House Keys." *Consumer Reports.* January 1985, 4.

Zara, Louis. *Locks and Keys.* New York: Walker and Company, 1969.

Index